40 ACRES

Warren Bull

Nine Bridges Press
Portland, Oregon

Also by Warren Bull, an Active Member of Mystery Writers of America and a Lifetime Member of Sisters in Crime with no hope of parole.

Novels
Abraham Lincoln for the Defense
Abraham Lincoln in Court and Campaign
Heartland
Death Deferred

Short Story Collections
Manhattan Mysteries
No Happy Endings
Killer Eulogy and Other Stories

History
Abraham Lincoln: Seldom Told Stories

40 ACRES
By Warren Bull
Copyright ©2022 by Warren Bull
All rights reserved
Nine Bridges Press
Portland, Oregon

Cover art credits: Public Domain

AWARDS

Derringer Flash Fiction Award finalist 2012
Young Adult Discovery Award for Novels finalist 2010
Best Short Story of the Year from the Missouri Writers' Guild 2006
Great Manhattan Mystery Conclave Short Story Award 2008
Alfred Hitchcock Magazine Mysterious Photograph Award Jan/Feb 2011
Cover Story and Editor's Choice in *Flash Bang Mysteries 2015* (The first issue of the magazine)
Strange Summer Mysteries Best Fantasy 2012
Strange Mysteries 4 Best Story 2012
Strange Mysteries Readers' Favorite Story 2009
Medium of Murder Finalist National Best Books 2008 (An award for the entire anthology that included a short story by Warren Bull)

CHAPTER ONE

I awoke in confusion. I felt the usual sensations that follow time travel — a fading memory of dreaming that I was flying, the taste of grapefruit on my tongue, and tingling in my fingertips and toes. But something felt very wrong. Where was I? When was I? My mission was to help Dolly Madison haul valuables out of the White House before the British set it on fire. The major American treasure I was sent to protect was, of course, Dolly herself. I expected to be in the city of Washington on August 24, 1814.

Instead, I found myself in the wrong place at the wrong time. I lay concealed in dense underbrush, wearing a green uniform like ten other soldiers around me. They were cursing the colonists revolting against their rightful king. Their accents and vocabulary sounded like the English working class in the late 1700s.

The commander, a man with bright red hair, snarled at us, "Shut your bone boxes." He was clearly Scottish.

I held an amazingly sophisticated breech-loading flintlock weapon with a rifled barrel. That plus the appearance of the commander let me guess the time and place. I remembered that in late 1777, or maybe it was 1778, Major Patrick Ferguson, a Scotsman, known as the finest shot in the British army, commanded a small force of expert marksmen. To locate colonial forces, they took cover close to Brandywine Creek in Pennsylvania where they could monitor a major roadway.

1

My memory proved correct when a cavalry officer dressed in the flamboyant uniform of a European hussar rode into view. He was followed by an American officer wearing a high-cocked hat. The British soldiers had no way of knowing who the men were, but I knew — Count Casimir Pulaski from Poland and General George Washington.

Ferguson signaled for me and two other men to move forward. One fellow moved with the grace of a serpent, not disturbing the underbrush or giving any hint of his passage. The second man grimaced and moved stiffly, as though in pain. His face was bruised. Without orders he got into a shooting position. I slid next to the second man and pulled his hand away from the rifle. He stared at me and struggled to free his hand. I held it immobile, ignoring the sounds of hoofbeats nearby.

"Don't move, Aevum," I whispered. "You're injured. You couldn't take me if you weren't. You cannot both fight me and carry out your assignment. Your opportunity is gone."

His eyes narrowed, but he did not move. Ferguson motioned us to return to our original places. As we made our way back, Ferguson stood. He shouted at the colonial officer. Washington looked back. He touched his hat in respect before cantering slowly away. Ferguson spared Washington's life. In the near future Pulaski would also save the future president.

The would-be assassin and I remained locked in that moment while time continued for the soldiers. From their point of view, we had never been there.

"Tempus Pilgrim," hissed the would-be assassin. "You cannot protect the American status quo against the will of the people. Your reluctance to spill blood leaves you weak and useless."

"The status quo is change," I said. "Painfully slow change, I admit. The wealthy continue to get richer and try to lock out the have-nots. We work with time to improve the state of the nation. Violence only begets more violence. The person who hates his slumlord and sets his apartment building on fire might hurt the building's owner financially, but he definitely hurts all who live there."

The revolutionist smiled. "If it hurts enough, the residents join our cause."

2

I shook my head. "Except various Aevum groups have different goals. You squabble over trivial disagreements, while big issues get ignored."

He did not respond.

I continued. "Your numbers are dwindling. How many set out on this mission? You made it through, but you were injured in the process. You probably won't make it back. Besides, what would killing Washington accomplish? Was there some plan past that? Change might make things even worse."

"Fine words," he spat. "Maybe not entirely false. Five of us were willing to give up our lives. You lose people too. What does your way accomplish beyond delaying real change?"

I thought about the Pilgrims on the Edmund Pettis Bridge in Selma, Alabama, on Bloody Sunday in 1965. Did our sacrifices add anything to the courage and dignity of those who tried to cross?

"Tell me, Tempus, would you have killed me back there if I had aimed at Washington?"

Time intervened. We were swept apart before I could answer. His image evaporated in front of me.

Of course, no two people experience time travel the same way. I never remember thoughts, sounds, or sights. For me, after a short period of disorientation and queasiness, it feels sort of like swimming. Instinctively, I ease into the current, which carries me along and deposits me safely, tired but exhilarated. The landing pad is a comfortable room in the secret army base where images of fish swim along the walls and American folk music plays softly from ceiling speakers.

I awoke stretched out on the familiar faded tan lounge chair. My clothing had not survived to modern times, just as all items from the present revert to the raw form they had in the past. But I wasn't thinking about that. I rushed to the door and opened it.

"I need to debrief ASAP," I yelled as I headed toward officer territory.

Second Lieutenant Margaret O'Donnell saw me coming and eyed me up and down. Seeing her in uniform was more than reason enough for any man to enlist. In that moment, however, I realized I had forgotten to put on a robe. I blushed.

"Any time you want me for a close personal inspection, Margaret, just let me know. Right now, I've gotta see the C.O."

Doctor Nasser, who had been alerted by the noise, appeared in the hall and grabbed my arm. "What happened, Ben?" Doc sounded even more pissed off than usual. I looked up at him. He was ten inches taller than me. He leaned down, looking at me like a gaunt hawk watching a sparrow.

"I went on one mission but ended up on another in an entirely different time and place. I stopped an Aevum revolutionist from killing George Washington."

"Completely impossible. Tell me exactly what happened."

"Other people need to know too. Let me borrow your cell phone. The General needs to find out."

A couple hours later, fully dressed this time, I walked toward the conference room. I stopped at the wall of honor commemorating each Pilgrim who died on a mission. I knew them all. I stopped before each photo, remembering them in a way very few people could. I was the last active Pilgrim of the first group trained. Four people left the program to do other things. Five were on the wall. Twelve people who trained after I did were also memorialized there.

Major General Wayne Porter, who ran the meeting, looked more like a reference librarian than a stereotypical general. He was a thin man with wire-rimmed glasses and a soft voice. His café au lait skin color showed his mixed ancestry.

"Thank you for your report, Ben. It seems to me that you've answered all the questions you could answer. As I told you before this mission, you are officially retired as a Pilgrim. Under no circumstances will you go on another mission."

I tried to speak, but he interrupted me.

"My decision is final. I've let you talk me into sending you back in a crisis way too many times. You're a civilian so I cannot give you orders, but the rest of the staff answers to me directly. You are now an instructor. Your personal experience will be invaluable in training others."

I knew I'd been playing Russian roulette and that I was lucky to have survived but living on the razor's edge had allowed me to feel my life more intensely. Retiring sounded terrible.

4

"Now to other matters," said the man in charge. "Dr. Nasser has asked to address the group. Most of you know that Matthew Nasser, M.D., Ph.D., deserves credit for developing time travel."

"Sir...." Nasser frowned.

"Doctor, I know you credit others for their contributions. But you were the person who put the pieces together and made it work."

Raising his eyebrows, Nasser glanced at me.

"You all know I was a revolutionist," said Nasser. "I helped write the equations and build the machines to pierce the flow and send people back through time. I was angry at what I saw as the American Dream being denied to minorities and immigrants. When I started to share my anger online, I found others who wanted to overthrow the powers that be. I wrote an aggressive equation that stabbed at the present and forced an opening so that people could claw through time to the past. I intended to use brute force to make American culture live up to its ideals."

He closed his eyes. Porter glanced at his watch and opened his mouth. I shook my head. The general stayed silent.

"I was naïve," said the doctor. "Violence begets violence. Islamic clerics declared me a traitor to my faith. They pronounced a fatwa; I am to be killed when they locate me. Dozens died before I saw the truth. Perhaps hundreds have died since. We tried to compel time to do our bidding through violence. How arrogant we were. How stupid. I betrayed the brave men and women who risked their lives for their beliefs.

"I brought everything I knew to Tempus. I expected to be executed for my crimes, but you showed me mercy. Your scientists showed me how they cooperate with time. No coercion. They work toward time's goals. I still want America to change faster than it does, but time moves as time moves."

Porter took off his glasses and polished them as he spoke. "Doctor, you discovered how we could travel in time. You improved our equations. Time reacted to the attacks from the initial approach. It improved its defenses. Revolutionists believing time was an enemy made themselves into time's enemy. Every attack resulted in better countermeasures that are increasingly dangerous to instigators. Time does not bend easily toward chaos. Attacks that fail cannot be repeated.

"We estimate the Aevum success rate of accessing the past is now down to under ten percent and falling rapidly. Of those who reach the past, virtually none of them return to the present. We are successful in attaining a time and place with a failure rate just above ten percent. Of course, we have no control over what happens during a mission, but our operatives almost always achieve their goals. We now recover everyone who manages to survive a mission."

"But I have so much to atone for," said the doctor. "I know I am impatient and impossible to please, but there must be more I can do. Whatever the risk, I want to go on a mission."

"You know the problems with that," said O'Donnell. "We've learned from harsh experience that we lose Pilgrims who don't blend in exceptionally well with the people of the era they enter. Even with their extensive research, unremarkable appearance, and careful speech patterns, they can easily stand out. We send them into inherently dangerous situations. Despite our best efforts some of them die." She glanced at me.

"Look at Ben, Doctor. He's five feet five inches tall and immensely strong. His coloring and features blend in. He's a talented linguist and a master at improvisation. You're six feet four inches tall. You have a beard, and your face is distinctive."

"You mean I look like a brute," said Nasser. "I know how ugly I am."

"You admit you are more obsessive than flexible," said the lieutenant. "You think profoundly but not rapidly. Perhaps we could manage to insert you into a particular time and place once, but you would never return. More than twenty of our people went on missions to the past and never came back."

"Doc, I know you're willing to die," said the general. "But we need you here to figure out why, for the first time ever, a Pilgrim who was prepared for one mission ended up with a different one."

"Time is not God," said Nasser. "Time does not assign missions. We do. Time cannot intervene directly with individuals."

I piped up, "I know, but God is greater than our understanding of the Divine. Perhaps time is a part of God. Maybe when there is a great need Allah works through an individual person such as he did with the prophet Muhammad."

Porter cleared his throat. "Our intelligence operatives report increasing chaos and reluctance to carry out missions by Aevum groups. The groups are turning on each other in frustration over their inability to accomplish anything in the past. The good news is that only a few isolated and hardened radicals are willing to even try any more. The bad news is that we can no longer infiltrate groups to discover the plans of those solitary few."

"What if time is now virtually free from attacks?" asked O'Connell. "Is it possible that it has become aware and active enough to independently push toward changes it desires?"

I sat back in my chair, thinking she could be onto something extremely important. If time could try to change anything in American history, what would it attempt to alter? And how?

CHAPTER TWO

I woke up perplexed. I had a fading memory of dreaming about flying, my tongue held the taste of grapefruit, and my fingertips and toes tingled. I must have time traveled but without preparation. No launch pad with scientists monitoring computers. No sophisticated mechanism nicknamed Mr. Peabody's Wayback Machine. Time plucked me from the meeting and dropped me...when and where?

I found myself driving a polished black barouche carriage pulled by a matched team of elegant black Canadian Pacers.

"Damn it, Time," I muttered. "You give me clothing, a carriage, and horses. Would it be so hard to include a newspaper?" I could figure this out. I was fashionably dressed in new clothing. From my recollection of paintings and early forms of photography, I guessed the clothes fit roughly the period from the 1850s through the 1880s. Due to my preparations for the Dolly Madison mission, it was easy to recognize that I was in the busy streets of Washington City. It was a later edition of the Washington than the British had plundered. The Smithsonian tower showed damage from a fire recent enough that only preliminary repairs had been made. The Capitol Dome was visible, and the bright copper Statue of Freedom on top was so new that it had not yet acquired a patina.

Unfortunately, I didn't know enough history for that to be definitive. Soldiers dressed in blue Union uniforms moved purposefully through the streets. Okay, that meant post-1861. Quite a few of the soldiers were Black, and white civilians seemed used to seeing Black soldiers. Therefore, it had to be later than the middle of 1862, probably later than 1863. People seemed in a celebratory mood, which was unusual during the terrible Civil War until close to the very end. Putting it all together had to be....

Time slowed. Events that happened in seconds rolled by in what I experienced as slow motion. Nasser suddenly appeared inside the carriage, dressed in an ill-fitting black suit. A handsome man sprang to the side of the carriage, extended a derringer inside, and shot the doctor in his temple.

The shooter whirled to the ground, shouting, "Sic semper tyrannis!" It was all very dramatic until I flung myself from the carriage to smash my boots into the back of John Wilkes Booth's head. We both landed in the mud. He shook me off with ease. He rose to his feet and swung at me. I ducked his jab. I kicked the side of his knee. He staggered, but, instead of falling, he lurched toward me and lit into me like a champion boxer. He ignored my feeble attempts at defense and smashed repeated punches into my ribs. I doubled over in pain.

Someone shouted, "He killed the President!"

Men and soldiers came running.

"Murderer!" I yelled. Someone shoved me aside. A wave of pain swept through my body as I fell back against a carriage wheel.

Surrounded now by a throng of angry, cursing men, Booth struggled, momentarily freeing himself from two soldiers before he was knocked to the ground.

I bent forward, breathing hard and bruised. A few feet away, two men removed the doctor's body from the carriage seat and placed it on a stretcher. I looked at the doctor's face as the men carried him away.

"My passenger looks like Old Abe, but thank God, he was not the President," I gasped. No one seemed to hear me.

In a moment time might sweep me away again. I wonder if it would return me to the landing pad in whatever the present is now. But Nasser.... Would there even be a landing pad anymore? With Nasser gone, I doubt it. Does the Tempus Pilgrims program even exist?

I looked around at where I was. Where I am. Where I'm likely to remain.

There will be a lot to do in this time to make Reconstruction work better after the Civil War ends than it did in my time flow. And there are certain to be more assassination attempts on the sixteenth president. Maybe I can do some good here. Maybe there is something even farther back in the past that I can help time with. I'm looking forward to the future — my future, whatever it may be.

. . .

The four mules pulling my wagon slowed and stopped on their own. The dog on the seat next to me growled and stared toward the dirt road in front of us. I couldn't see anything unusual in the open area ahead but I knew something dangerous was on the way. Dogs can smell what's coming a lot better than humans. The mules had been in the Union Army before I got them. They had developed a sense for when something was wrong. I would be a fool to ignore them. Fools did not live long in these parts in Georgia. I stopped and reached behind my seat for a second 1858 Remington revolver to back up the one I carried strapped on my hip. I put the revolver on the seat beside me.

In a minute a young Black man strode quickly out of the trees and then up the road toward me. He looked back over his shoulder once or twice, each time increasing his pace. As he neared, I could see that he was broad-shouldered and handsome. He might have been descended from an African king. He stumbled as he approached and dropped to one knee.

"Why you here?" he gasped, his chest heaving. His bright blue embroidered shirt was plastered with sweat to his body. His tan trousers were damp and dirty; his boots, worn.

He would never believe me if I told him. In fact, I was not certain myself why time or something related to time had snatched me from the distant future and dropped me into that evening when Abraham Lincoln had gone to Ford's Theater. I helped stop Booth, but then I was never snatched back to the landing pad. Instead, I stayed stuck. I worked for the man known as the Great Emancipator through the rest of the Civil War and his second full term in office. I was now determined to help President Grant see that Sherman's Special Field Order No. 15, known in my time as "40 Acres and a Mule," were enforced long enough to give the newly emancipated people a chance at a better life. In this time stream, like my old one, there were simply not enough mules for everyone who wanted one.

"I'm just an honest man at work," I said. "I stopped, sensing that trouble might be coming. My best guess is that the trouble is hot on your trail."

"White ratbags claim...." He stopped to catch his breath. "Too friendly... white girl. Ain't so." He took a moment before continuing. "She teased me.... My shirt." He swayed but rose to his feet. "Dint mean nothin' by it. Guess I shouldn't'a spoke."

"How many are there after you?" I asked.

"Her daddy. His boys. Six all told," he said. His breathing was close to normal. "They all got horses. You gotta help me. You lighter skinned, so you takin' a chance. They might not be happy just nailin' my hide to the barn. Please. "

"I'll help," I said. "But only if you do exactly what I tell you. I will not die for you today. I have too many important things to do. If you prove to be too full of yourself to bother with, I swear to God I will drive off and leave you to them."

He nodded.

"First, take off that pretty shirt and throw it so far away it can't be seen from the road."

"My woman made that special," he protested.

"And I'm sure your corpse would look good in it," I said. "If you want my help and want to live, you have to make it hard for them to recognize you." I snapped the reins. The mules stepped forward.

"Hold on," he said. He stripped off the shirt and threw it hard. It disappeared into a mucky gully on the side of the road.

I stopped the wagon. "Now, roll in the dirt and rub some mud on your pretty face."

He did without comment.

"Next, climb up here."

He grabbed the seat, pulled himself up and sat down beside me. He smelled foul. I pulled off my hat and handed it to him.

"Good. Now put this on. Slouch forward, keep your eyes down,

11

and don't talk."

Six hard-favored men came into view riding raw-boned horses.

He started, "Thank you–"

I interrupted him. "Don't say a word. They could recognize your voice."

The men pulled up and stopped about five yards away.

"Would you gentlemen kindly stay where you are, please?" I asked. "I get nervous when strangers surround me." I waited while they looked me over, no doubt aware that my revolvers could hold two bullets for each of them.

The tallest of them of them spat. "Do you think we're here to steal your mules?"

"You wouldn't be the first, sir," I answered. "I still got them, though, and I plan to keep them. But I mean no offense. How may I be of service to you?"

The oldest member of the group said, "We're lookin' for a young colored buck named Raymond. Some'd say he is good lookin'. He wears a fancy blue shirt and struts around like a rooster. You see anyone like that pass by?"

"No, sir," I said. "Nobody passed by for quite some time. I assure you, that is the truth."

The man continued, looking at Raymond. "You see anyone?"

Unobtrusively, I elbowed Raymond in his ribs when I turned toward him. Raymond shook his head, looking down.

One of the boys said, "Maybe he's hiding in your wagon."

"No, sir," I answered. "I would know, and being an honest man, I would tell you. Nobody's there. There isn't much back there but boxes. It's not covered. You could see him if he was trying to hide there."

The older man spoke again. "If you see him, tell him we won't forget."

"Sorry, sir, but I never met this Raymond," I said. "If I run across a young Black man and he says he's Raymond, I will tell him.... Who should I say won't forget him?"

"I'm Evander Dickenson. These are my sons. Raymond was too free in gabbin' with my daughter."

"If I see him, I will tell him, sir," I said. "I hope your daughter is safe."

"Don't trouble yourself, boy. Don't need any coloreds even thinkin' about her. It'll be a long time afore she goes around by herself again."

The smallest rider spoke up. "Who's that ridin' with you? How long he been in your wagon?"

I looked in Raymond's direction. "This Darkee's been riding with me for weeks," I said. My dog jumped into my lap and looked up at me. "With your permission, sir, I'd like to get on with my travels."

"Time's a wastin', boys," said Dickenson. The men spread out, and I drove between them. They watched as my wagon rolled on slowly. The mules wanted to get away from the Dickensons nearly as much as I did, but I kept the reins tight to keep the pace down. When we were about ten yards past, I heard the men ride on.

Raymond glanced back at them. After another five minutes he spoke.

"They ain't comin' this way," he sighed.

"You did good," I said. "Sorry if I was abrupt. There was no time for a long explanation."

"You prob'ly already guessed. I'm Raymond," he said. He extended his hand, and I shook it.

"Pleased to meet you, Raymond. I'm Ben. I promised a man named Evander Dickenson that if we met, I would tell you he won't forget you. I'd take that as a threat."

"I knew that," said Raymond.

"I know you did," I said. "But I made Dickenson a promise. I'm an honest man." My dog sniffed Raymond. Apparently, he approved of my new passenger. I scratched the dog's ear. "You did good too. You're a good dog, Darkee. A very good dog."

. . .

Raymond squirmed in his seat and frowned. I wondered why a man who had just avoided dying looked as worried as he did.

"The wife ain't gonna be happy with how I look. She made that shirt special for me. I went and chucked it in a ditch."

I nodded.

"I 'preciate what you did for me. I'd be dead if you hadn't helped. It'd be nice if you'd share a meal and spend the night with us. And, uh, maybe you'd be willin' to tell Lilly what happened to my shirt?"

"Thanks," I answered. "Somebody else's cooking will be a welcome change. Whereabouts do you live?"

"We're headed right toward my place," he said. "We live on a farm in that great long strip of land on the coast. Land used to belong to the Whites. We call it Beulah Land 'cause it's as close to heaven as colored folk can get on this earth. Whites call it Sherman's Shore."

"Good," I said. "That's just where I'm heading. Tell me, when the Dickensons were chasing you, why didn't you hightail it there? Aren't there colored troops assigned to protect the people in that area?"

"Yes, sir, but it's a lot of land for the troops to cover.," he said. "The White commanding officer, Capt'n March, tol' us to not start any trouble. Seems like any trouble comes along, he thinks we brung it. And I dint want a passel of armed angry white men ridin' up on my family."

"I'm curious," I said. "Are there other problems in Beulah Land?"

"Nothin' serious. We all get along and help each other. I'd feel better if the capt'n let us to keep enough weapons to defend ourselves. He locked up most of what we had in the armory. He says it's the gov'ment's job to protect us. I spose that's so, but we don't feel safe."

"Lots of land and not so many soldiers," I said. "I don't believe I've heard of Captain March before."

"His uncle was a general. Least that's what the soldiers say. But Capt'n was in Washington City all the way through the war. The soldiers don't think much of him and he knows it. He's always throwin' his weight around, favorin' the Whites over us." Raymond tipped his head back. "Don't get me wrong. We're lucky to get a chance here. Ain't nobody gonna rock the boat, seein' as how deep the water is."

"Are there other officers?" I asked.

"Two lieutenants. Reynolds and Franks. They help us when they

14

can. Reynolds helps as much as he can."

We rode in silence as I mulled over what Raymond had said. Soon we came to a simple fence that lined the road on the inland side. Rails were stacked one on another in a zig-zag pattern. Only gravity kept them together. Around here it was called a snake fence.

"This's the boundary of Beulah Land," said Raymond. "Everythin' from here to the sea is ours. Nobody has claimed this piece. Too close to the edge, I reckon."

"Too hard to clear the thick pine forest, maybe," I answered. "It looks like the trees have been growing for years and the underbrush is tangled. It's kind of a natural defense barrier. A man could hack his way through, but not easily or quickly."

"They put a sentry post up ahead a ways, in more of a break in the trees," said Raymond.

Before long I spotted a rustic building positioned on a rise outside the forest. It had an unfinished look to it, more like a temporary shelter than a place people planned to live in for years to come. The mules slowed.

"Better get your mules to movin' afore they spot us," warned Raymond.

I didn't take the time to ask questions. I snapped the reins and yelled, "Git!"

The mules took off like a locomotive, throwing up dirt with their hooves. I heard a shot. A puff of dust rose from far to the left. I could see a sturdier building ahead.

"That weren't the outpost. Up ahead, that's the outpost," said Raymond. "Once we git there we'll be out of their range."

When we reached the outpost, I pulled beyond it and stopped the wagon. A heavyset Black trooper came out of the building. I recognized him: Mica.

"Speak of the devil, and he appears," Mica shouted. "We was just talkin' about you, Ben. How you been?"

A bullet whistled by. Raymond flinched and hopped out of the wagon. He ran toward the building to put it between him and the shooters. Darkee looked at him and then at me and then lay down in the wagon behind the seat. The dog had been in enough firefights to recognize when it was time to move quickly and when it was not.

"Don't worry about the shootin', young'un," said Mica, trying to put Raymond's mind at ease. "They're terrible shots. They've been sendin' bullets our direction for months now and they never come close. The only way they could kill us is to bore us to death. I'm too old and too stiff to be hoofin' when I don' need to."

"Mica, even a blind hog finds an acorn once in a while," I said. "Who's shootin' at us?"

"Capt'n says they're outlaws, not from around here," said Raymond.

"No matter what he says, I recognize the Harkrader brothers, Clem and Dill," said Mica. "They have to be shooting from at least 700 yards away. My Springfield isn't accurate past 500 yards. Even those jackanapeses might put a bullet in me before I got close enough to drill 'em."

A tall, thin dark-skinned man walked out of the building.

"You remember Click Duncan," Mica said.

"I certainly do. Best telegraph operator I ever knew."

"I ain't the quickest on the key," said Click.

"No, but I've never known you to make a mistake, even under fire," I answered.

"That don't help much right now. I can't shoot as well as Mica."

"Are they ever gonna stop shootin' at us?" asked Raymond from the side of the building.

"They usually don't stop until we go inside," said Mica. "They occasionally hit the barn over there when they aim at us."

"By the sound those bullets make, those no-account greybacks have a Whitworth," I said.

"What's that?" asked Raymond.

"The best rifle in the world," I answered. "The Confederates had very few and they gave them only to the very best marksmen. Those two don't know how to use it or we'd all be dead. They don't deserve a beautiful weapon like that. How did a pair of idiots end up with it, I wonder?"

"So, what're you gonna do about it?" Raymond asked.

"I believe I will take it from them," I said. I climbed into the back of the wagon and pried open a long crate. I took out a breech-loading Sharps with a double-set trigger and handed it to Mica. I took another for myself. I could see them waving their hats and pointing at us. They did not take cover. Apparently, they thought the idea of us shooting back was funny.

I walked Mica through the simple process of loading the Sharps. I loaded mine and two others, hoping we could get four shots off quickly if we need to.

"The gun is sighted well," I said. "The wind will have a little bit more of an effect than when you shoot at 500 yards and gravity will pull it down a little more, but not much. Don't try anything fancy. Just aim for the center of the body."

"How 'bout if you go first?" asked Mica. "I can see how you aim and what happens to your shot before I try."

"Good idea," I said. "If I hit one, the other one will probably freeze for a moment."

For stability I rested my Sharps on the edge of the wagon. As the breeze began to die down, the rifle became part of my body. I concentrated on the man in the distance and visualized how the shot would go. The outlaw became just a target, not a human being. My body became stable but not rigid. I calmed myself. After exhaling and between heartbeats I squeezed the trigger. I felt the recoil at the same time I heard the shot and saw white smoke. One of the brothers collapsed backwards, blood spurting from his face. I handed my rifle to Click to reload and grabbed one of the loaded Sharps from him. Mica fired. The other Harkrader spun and dropped. I caught a slight smell like charcoal.

"He ain't dead, not like the one you shot," said Mica.

"Great shooting with a rifle you never used before," I said. I repeated the actions I had taken before and waited for the smoke to dissipate. I shot the twitching body in the head. It stopped moving.

"Now they're both dead," said Click. "Devil man, don't you ever come huntin' me. Jest tell me and I will kill myself to save you the trouble."

"If that don't beat all!" said Raymond. "I never saw shootin' like that."

"Maybe you never saw a Sharps rifle before," Click said to Raymond. "They used to say a man was a Sharps shooter afore they came up with the word sharpshooter. Ben is a man for all seasons. He saved

President Lincoln's life."

"He won't tell you on his own, but you gotta give the devil his due," said Mica. "Ben's the devil you want on your side. He'll bring down hell on the other side."

"You two prattle on like old ladies at a church supper," I said. "The truth is that five years ago, I drove a carriage with a passenger who looked like the former president. John Wilkes Booth shot the man and crowed that he killed Lincoln. I distracted Booth by getting the tar beat out of me until a squad of bluebellies piled on top of him and took him down. Later, he and his crew dangled from the gallows for their plans. Even though Booth nearly beat me to death, Lincoln's favorite marshal, Ward Hill Lamont, hired me to help guard Mr. Lincoln for the rest of his term. There were other assassination attempts. I was more help with them. That's all."

"That's all?" asked Click. "Raymond, do you imagine you'd have an inch of land for your own self if Lincoln had been killed? Andrew Johnson would never have gone for it. You wouldn't be a citizen or be able to vote. Lincoln got all that for us. Booth apart, Ben kept Lincoln alive so's he could do it."

"Enough chin wagging," I said. "Mica, let's go check on your shooting and see what kind of rifles those bushwhackers had."

"Can I come too?" asked Raymond.

"Why don't you make yourself useful here?" I asked. "You're young and strong. I bet old Click can find something for you to do. This is a great place for the post. It's a natural chokepoint. Any force has to pass by closely. They've been guarding you. You might do some work to make this place safer. It would help them and help you too."

CHAPTER THREE

As we rode out in the wagon, Mica asked, "How is Mr. Lincoln?"

"He's become an old man, my friend. I don't think he's long for this world. His poor wife is not altogether sane. She worries all the time that somebody plans to kill him even though he's out of office. She can't shake the needless worry that she'll be penniless after he dies."

Mica shook his head. "Sad. Newspapers north and south took turns havin' at her. They never wrote about her visitin' wounded men or givin' money to escaped slaves."

"She did it and never called attention to herself," I said. "The deaths of her sons broke her mind and spirit."

The mules slowed as they reached the place where the men's bodies lay. The Whitworth rested on the ground next to the man I shot.

Mica whistled. "Looky there. You got him right 'tween the eyes."

"That wasn't my particular target," I said. "I just shot at his head."

A box of about thirty hexagonal cartridges sat on the ground next to the body. A smaller box held everything else needed. I examined the weapon.

"No wonder those crackers couldn't shoot straight," I said. "The barrel is filthy."

The second body had a wound high on the right shoulder and another just above the left ear.

Mica frowned. "Tarnation, he might've survived the busted shoulder."

"No, without a doctor on the spot, he would have bled out sooner or later. He would have died even if my shot had missed. However, if he was tough as an old boot, he might have been able to shoot back once or twice."

I looked at the dwelling.

"I thought this was just a shack, but it's solidly built," I said.

"They've been usin' it for about three months now," said Mica. "Somebody's there all the time. They come in shifts of two or three. It must be about time for the next group."

"Let's mess up their plans," I said.

Mica smiled.

Inside the building were beds and furnishings: wool blankets, a solid table, tin plates, and utensils. An oil lantern hung on a wire from the ceiling. Candle lanterns sat on shelves with lucifers, alongside playing cards, dice, and an earthenware jug. A smoked butchered hog hung from the ceiling.

"I've seen lots of places worse than this," said Mica.

"Let's load what we want onto the wagon. I see horses in the corral. I'll search the bodies for anything else. They won't need it."

After we collected everything we wanted, Mica said, "We should we burn this place."

"Yes, and the bodies too. Let their people wonder what happened to them."

I found a bottle of oil for the lamp and poured some on the floor and roof. I splashed moonshine from the jug over the bodies. From outside the door I lit a lucifer and tossed it inside. The fire started with a whoosh. I felt the heat instantly. Flames roared as they climbed to the roof. After a few minutes the building collapsed in on itself. Noise from the fire died down to crackling as we headed back toward the outpost.

"So, this captain, Captain March, just let them stay there and shoot at you?" I asked.

"He said he didn't reckon they'd hit us. He kept promisin' to send out a patrol to scare 'em off, but he never got around to it. Just like he never got around to connectin' the sentry post to the telegraph."

"So, what were you supposed to do if you got attacked?"

Mica spat. "I reckon we were sposed to kill 'em all first and report it second."

"Well, after the other Harkraders find their place burned and two bodies in the ashes, they'll likely respond. I hope I didn't get you in Dutch."

"I was tired of gettin' shot at and doin' nothin' about it," said Mica.

"You'll have the Whitworth, plenty of bullets and I can give you a couple of Sharps too," I said. "You'll be able to even the odds a bit before they get close enough to hit you."

"If they attack from the south," said Mica.

"They're not likely to come in from the ocean. An amphibious assault is hard to pull off. Too much can go wrong. Well-trained troops could do it, but disorganized groups could not. The northern border is protected by war-hardened soldiers from the next section of Sherman's Shore. Some are veterans of the 54th Massachusetts Volunteer Infantry. Nobody in their right mind would mess with them. They keep a sharp eye on their southern end. I thought the forest was strong enough by the outpost to keep them from coming in from the west."

"It is here. But it thins out as you go north. When we can, we work on gettin' a staked fence over a stone wall for defense where it's needed, but there's a stretch farther north on a farm where you can walk right through the border, thanks to the capt'n," said Mica.

I shook my head. "I'm bound to butt heads with this captain of yours. Somebody had to be an excellent shot to get one of the few Whitworths those greybacks had. If they get through north of here, they can come at you from all directions. Whoever owns the Whitworth knows how to fight. I need to get to headquarters to untangle this knot."

"That's why you're here," said Mica as he climbed down from the wagon.

"Yes, President Grant sent me a letter with instructions that, once the Lincolns were settled in, I was to scout this part of the Sherman Shore and take whatever steps needed to bring Fort Abraham Galloway up to snuff. Every other settlement has been attacked. They all sent the attackers back dead or bloodied and regretful. He heard some strange things about weak borders and settlers' weapons being seized. Grant knows when apparent strength hides weakness. I've worked with him in the past. He trusts me."

"You'd best be gettin' along then," said Mica.

"I'm sorry I can't stay and help you with these outlaws," I said.

"Me and Click will manage. Raymond's pretty wife came out a day ago to see if he'd been by. Lilly is nearly as white as the flower she's named after. She cracks the whip in that family."

Click said he knew just the man in the Washington City War Department who could get a message to the president without delay. I left it to him to compose the telegraph about conditions in Beulah Land. I couldn't tell him my plans because I didn't have them figured out.

Raymond climbed back onto the wagon, and he and Darkee and I set out along the road that stayed close to the border. For some distance the fence was staked over a stone wall. It would not stop an invasion by itself, but it would take time and effort to breach. A few defenders could stop superior numbers in those places. Eventually we came to the break in the wall Mica told me about. A patch of land had been planted with corn that had grown to a height of five feet. A corner of the field extended into Sherman's Shore about fifteen feet. A ruddy-faced young man with a hoe was digging out weeds. He looked up at our approach.

"There's no need to look so angry, friend," he said to me. "What did corn ever do to thee?"

"It's not the corn," I said. "It's where the corn is planted. Somebody took down the wall that marks the edge of Sherman's Shore. It's on land Congress gave to us."

The man grimaced. "I was afraid of that. I should never have trusted that old Reb. He had a map and he claimed he owned this ground. I should have been more careful. My name is Jacob Ashmore. My wife, Ruth, and I are Quakers. We came here to teach and help the formerly enslaved people. A captain came by, but he didn't object."

"That capt'n and Ben here are gonna have it out," said Raymond. "I wanna see that."

"You meant no harm," I said. I thought for a moment. "I can't pay you for land you don't own, but I can buy your crops. What do you reckon the corn on this side of the fence is worth?"

He rubbed his chin. "The corn plus the work I put in, maybe a quarter at most."

"Tell you what, "I said. "There's a chance some yahoos might come raiding soon. I expect they know about the breach, and I don't have enough time now to stay and put the wall back up. If you agree to put it back and make it strong enough to slow them down, I'll give you three dollars in silver."

"They'd likely ride right through the corn before they see the fence," he said. "For three dollars I can build thee a horse-tight chest-high wall the ruffians'll regret not knowing about. Watching that would be more fun than a circus. I'll get right to it."

Jacob stuck out his hand and we shook on the deal. Few White men would have offered to shake hands with me.

We had not traveled much farther when we met colored troops on the road. Two men, Jeremiah and Jefferson, who looked like brothers, hailed us.

"They say you never have to call for the devil. He's already here," called out Jeremiah.

"But they don't say he travels with a peacock," said Jefferson, laughing.

I could see a cart pulled by a donkey trailing unstrung telegraph wire and a wagon loaded with tall poles pulled by a draft horse. Half a dozen soldiers lounged around the scene. A young white officer wearing a lieutenant's uniform came forward.

"What are you men laughing at?" he demanded.

"Lieutenant Franks, you know how Raymond's wife likes to dress him up like a doll," said Jeremiah. "We take to callin' him a peacock 'cause he looks so pretty. I gotta admit, though, that if I had me a woman as pretty as her, I'd do 'bout any dog dang thing she wanted."

"That ordinary-lookin' fella next to him is the farthest thing from ordinary," said Jefferson. "His name is Ben Devlin. Mess with him and there'll be the devil to pay."

The lieutenant's head snapped toward me. His eyes widened.

"Shoot that man," he commanded.

The soldiers froze.

I waited a moment to calm myself before answering.

"That's not a good idea, lieutenant," I said. "My dog would miss me. Why do you want them to shoot me?"

"The captain gave strict orders," said Franks. "He said to be on the lookout for a dangerous spy who would claim to be Ben Devlin." He looked at his men. "Why doesn't anybody obey my order?" He sounded surprised. He reached for his weapon.

I reached for mine as well.

"Lieutenant, your holster is snapped shut," I said. "That keeps your gun in place while you ride, but it gives me so much time that I could kill you, bury you, and hold a memorial service over your grave before you get it free."

He put his hands up.

I closed my eyes for a few seconds and then opened them again. I looked hard at the officer, whose raised hands were trembling. "Of course the captain would order that. He couldn't directly order his men to shoot me, but he could create confusion and hope for the best. Lieutenant, you say the order was to shoot anybody who pretended he was Ben Devlin, right?"

He nodded.

"So, before you go and shoot me, which would end eventually with you hanging from a noose, consider. Did I claim to be Ben Devlin? Or did these men, who know me personally, identify me as the real Ben Devlin? Were your orders to watch out for the actual person and kill the real me? Or did the orders concern an imposter?"

"Upon consideration, I withdraw the order to shoot," said the officer. He lowered his arms.

"Thank you, sir. That is a relief," I said. "I have something to show you."

I retrieved a letter from my belongings. "I think you'll recognize the signature as President Grant's. To summarize briefly, he lists me as his personal representative. He informs the reader that any instructions I give are to be treated as an order from the president himself. My orders supersede orders from anyone other than the president himself. Do you agree?"

"Yes, sir," said Franks. "This is a most unusual situation."

"It is. When he wrote this letter, the President did not have any idea what was happening here. I'm sure he informed Captain March that I was coming to make an inspection. The commander knew the President was concerned and unhappy. Neither the President nor I suspected that the captain would take the opportunity to have me killed, as he obviously did. I appreciate your caution in obeying your superior's orders."

"The captain has been acting strange," said the officer. "He does not like being questioned. He's butted heads with Mr. Reynolds, who outranks me, more than with me. I've been trying to stay out of range, but some of the things the captain's done don't make any sense."

"Like what?" I asked.

"Like letting the outlaws establish a place on Sherman's Shore. Why hasn't he sent a force to get them out? And this detail. He ordered me to take the men and set up a telegraph office in Springfield, but Springfield is outside the border. The line doesn't go to the sentry post where it's needed the most. I admit I was going slow as molasses, but I was hoping the commander would come to his senses. We're supposed to go to the gap in the fence where the teachers live and string it from there to the town. But why allow a goldurn gap at all, and why make it go right where we're completely undefended?"

"It sounds like he's setting up an attack on his own men," I said. "I have new orders for you. I want your two strongest men to go ahead to Jacob and Ruth's farm and help Jacob complete the wall he's building. The rest can string the telegraph line as quickly as possible to the sentry post. I want you to locate Lieutenant Reynolds and tell him what you've seen without alerting the captain. Don't report in. Ask the men where Reynolds is and speak to him. Then go where he directs you."

"Yes, sir," said Franks.

"What can I do?" asked Raymond.

"I can't give you orders since you're a civilian, but I would be much obliged if you would hightail it back to Click and tell him about the captain trying to ambush me so he can get that information to Grant. The President may have to send a high-ranking officer if I get killed."

"You got the letter what puts you in charge," said the young man.

"Yes, but the captain's orders are to shoot on sight. I don't believe the letter would stop a bullet."

CHAPTER FOUR

I gave Raymond and two soldiers a ride back to my newly acquired corn field. Raymond took off toward the sentry post. The two soldiers, Silas and Noah, greeted Jacob.

"Professor Ashmore, I got hold of the whole dang alphabet now," said Silas.

Noah snickered. "He does, but he has his own kind of spellin'. And I can cypher better than him."

Silas and Noah assumed a mock boxing stance and laughed.

"Gentlemen, I am honored that you remember me and thy lessons. Have thee come for a refresher lesson?"

"You taught these men?" I asked.

"Pretty much the entire troop," answered Ashmore.

"Did you teach Raymond's wife too?" I asked.

"Ruth worked with her more than I did," he answered.

"Would it be possible for me to speak to your wife, sir?" I asked. "It might be important."

"Of course," he said. "I'll fetch her. Please call me Jacob, not sir."

While I waited, Silas and Noah competed to see who could put the heaviest stones into the fence and arrange them into a solid wall that would come chest-high on most horses. I pitched in for a bit, but they were both a lot stronger than I was. They laughed at my efforts.

Ruth Ashmore brought a bucket of water and a cup with her. The soldiers drank and joked with her husband while she and I talked.

My dog, who is a great judge of character, approached her, wagging his tail. She scratched him behind his ears and petted him. I introduced him to her.

"Why did thee choose such a terrible name for thy dog?" she asked.

"He is much slower to anger than I am. I have a bit of a temper. Sometimes people say things that would chap my hide if they were addressed to me. Those things don't bother my dog at all. So, I just keep in mind that the awful, insulting things they say are directed at my friend. He ignores them. The stupid people don't know Darkee at all. What they say about him is so ridiculous it's funny. That helps me stay calm. You're a big help, Darkee. You're such a good dog."

Darkee came to me, and I petted him.

Ruth giggled. "Just the same, I think I'll refrain from using that name."

"Thanks for speaking with me," I said. "Your husband said Lilly was your student. I'm trying to make sense of what's going on around here. I haven't met Lilly, but her name keeps popping up. I have the feeling that she is involved with this subversion of the settlement, although I cannot say why. Would you be willing to tell me about her?"

"The first thing thee will notice is that she is strikingly beautiful," said Ruth. "She is also brilliant. She learned to read and write more quickly than any student I've ever had. And God gifted her with an artist's ability to design dresses. She crafted two for me that I will never have an occasion grand enough to wear. Perhaps it was vanity to keep them, but she had striven so to produce them that I did not wish to discourage her. And, vain as it is, I sometimes imagine myself wearing one whilst among the famous people at a grand event. She would be in demand as a creator of fashionable gowns in a place where there are formal balls and high society events."

"Which does not describe Sherman's Shore," I said. "She seems out of place."

Ruth blinked and nodded. "I fear she has never fit in anywhere. Her mistress and master were not accepted by plantation society. Maybe because they were immigrants. I'm not sure. In grand plantations she would have been an ornamental house slave and had the chance to acquire some social skills by observing how the owners acted. Where she was, she worked in the fields. She had no education. Her beauty was more of a curse than a blessing, poor child. She attracted unwanted attention from men who, because she was a slave, she could not refuse. When I first met her, her speech was that of the most ignorant backwoods people. She had no acquaintance with even the rudiments of polite behavior."

"But she could design dresses?" I asked. "I can feel betrayal and slaughter in the air. I know a great deal starts with the captain, but it's like trying to put together a mosaic. There are odd pieces here and there."

"No, she could patch torn clothing and quilts," said the teacher. "I saw she had a sense of how colors could go together pleasingly, and she made wonderful tiny stitches. I encouraged her to expand her efforts. She had no concept of what she might become. Once she started to learn, she showed an unquenchable desire to better every aspect of her life. It was like she had a hunger that could not be satisfied. Her intensity was more than a little bit frightening. Thee might liken her to Paul on the road to Damascus. Once he saw the light, he was as relentless in sharing it as he had been in trying to extinguish it."

"Well, she certainly improved her life when she joined Raymond," I said.

"Yes, Raymond is a good man," said Ruth, frowning. "He is nearly as handsome as she is gorgeous, although he is more vain about his appearance than she is. They make a striking couple. He's strong enough to protect her from men who would abuse her."

"From your tone of voice, I get the idea that your statements should be followed by the word 'but'," I said. "Believe me, I have no intention of repeating what you tell me to anyone else. It sounds like Lilly is a remarkable person for what she has made of herself. Having come so far, she must have loftier ambitions."

I shook my head before continuing. "Mrs. Ashmore, I'm grasping at straws. I know a great deal starts with the captain, but this puzzle…. I am missing some important element. How can I spoil the plan without knowing what the plan is? I have a tingling in my mind that Lilly is involved. But to what end? How is she connected to the captain? Is she? What am I missing?"

"Friend Devlin, I wonder if thee truly understands how much a woman's existence is determined by the men in her life — her father, her husband, her sons. Would thee laugh at me if I say Mary Todd Lincoln had to submerge her own ambitions so they flowed through her husband? I can't help but wonder what the First Lady could have become given the chance."

"I wouldn't laugh, ma'am. I admit to having the same idea."

Ruth stared at me.

"Wherever art thee from, sir? Nowhere around here. Even my beloved Jacob whose heart shines with the light of God does not understand. I know naught of schemes. But I know Lilly. She has raised herself up by attaching to one man and then abandoning him for a different man with more promise. She doesn't so much plan it out as she recognizes an opportunity when it happens and snaps it up. I believe she is still uncertain of her own skills and desperate to rise any way she can. Understandably, she sees the world as unfair and thus has no hesitation to use and discard people around her."

Of course, the teacher had no idea where I was really from. I thought for a moment before I spoke.

"Where am I from? I am from a place so far away that I can never return to it. I suppose, like Lilly, that I will never entirely fit in. Your description of her almost sounds like a personal warning."

"It is, Friend Devlin. Thee would be a step up from Raymond."

I flinched.

"I don't understand," I said. "I am nowhere near as handsome or strong as he is."

"No, but thee obviously has had a better education. Thy skin is lighter. Thy facial features and hair don't absolutely label thee as colored like Raymond's do him. He might well be her best choice among local men of the Black race, but thee could open another door for her. You two could move to somewhere up north where nobody knows thee and appear as an immigrant family from Europe, say, Greece or Italy. Standing together you two would no longer be seen as unquestioningly colored. You two could pass as white."

My mind went blank for a moment, and then, without warning, ideas of all sorts came rushing in about opportunities I had not

30

dreamed possible in this timeline.

"Thee could transform thy life. And hers. I can see the idea surprises thee, but she will latch onto it and snap it up within seconds when she sees thee."

At that moment shots rang out. I yelled at the teacher to take cover. My training took over. I found myself scanning our surroundings, revolver already in hand even though I did not remember drawing it. I had time to aim like I was target shooting. Four men riding at a gallop came whooping and shooting at us through the corn field. I shot twice at where I thought the man closest to us would be when the bullets arrived. He leaned forward toward his horse's neck. I was gratified to see him fall from the saddle. A second man sat more erect in his saddle, probably intending to shoot from a more stable position. I shot once and saw a burst of red from the side of his head before he dropped. The last two were farther away, riding in zigzag patterns as they approached the newly built wall. Shots came from the soldiers behind the wall. One horse collapsed and rolled over its rider, apparently crushing the rider's chest with the saddle horn. The last attacker wheeled his horse around, still shooting. His body jerked. He fired once at nothing in particular. His second shot came close to hitting the teacher crouching next to me. Then I emptied my revolver in his direction. He slid off his horse.

Mrs. Ashmore trembled. Tears ran down her face.

"Did thee have to shoot the last man?" she asked.

"I'm sorry," I said, grimacing and looking away. "I'm sorry you had to see that. For the last five years, my job was to protect the President. A number of people tried to kill him from ambush. I learned to react by instinct, without stopping to think about it. It was necessary to protect him. He is a great man, but I need to overcome that reaction now."

She wiped at her tears. "But thee did not shoot him until after he shot close to us, did thee?"

I did not reply. I dropped the loading lever of my now-empty Remington, slid out the cylinder pin and removed the spent cylinder. The capped spare cylinder in my pocket was ready to explode. Each bullet could go off on its own like a small bomb. Despite hours and hours of practice, switching to a loaded cylinder always involved some degree of risk. After pocketing the old cylinder, I carefully slid the spare into the frame of the revolver. I rotated it slightly to get the alignment correct before sliding the pin back in. Then I put the loading lever back in place. My revolver had another full load of six shots. I did not have time to clean the weapon, but, because I used bullets with a special high-performance sporting-grade black powder, fouling was minimal and the revolvers could maintain their accuracy without cleaning longer than most.

Weapon in hand, I stepped cautiously toward the closest assailant, approaching from out of his possible line of sight. He was dead. When a man's spirit leaves the body, the remains look like they had never been alive. The man looked like an oversized puppet with the strings cut. His horse grazed nearby. I talked calmly to the animal. She stood quietly while I heaved the body onto her back. Using a rope from the saddle I bound his ankles to his wrists and then headed toward the second body.

The second horse was a younger stallion and a lot more skittish about toting a corpse. The presence of the mare calmed him down. He reluctantly allowed me to tie his former rider over his back. By the time I returned to where the teacher and I had been talking, the others were gathered with the two other bodies and the one remaining horse.

"I'm sorry about this tragedy," I said. "And I'm even more sorry that I need to go to the sentry post with Silas and Noah right away and leave all this mess to you."

"We have a wagon," said Ruth. "If thee would help load the departed into that, Jacob can finish the wall, I can help him bury the dead horse, and then we can take the men's bodies to the church in Springfield."

"I'm very much obliged, ma'am. We'll take the weapons and ammo from these poor souls so as to not re-arm our enemies. I can drive the mules, and these two can ride horses so we can get to the other soldiers sooner."

She nodded. It occurred to me that some heroes shun violence but show as much bravery as any soldier on earth. Unarmed, the Ashmores had come to this blood-soaked land to help people who others regarded as less than fully human. They knew they would be looked down on, even despised. They knew people had been murdered for less than what they openly acknowledged they intended to do. Quietly they set to work, doing as much as anyone else to bend the world toward justice and peace without condemning people who did not dare to live up to their standards. I on the other hand had sought out the best weapons, powder, and training to gain every possible advantage over my enemies before I came here. I didn't have the gumption to trust my faith alone.

We needed to go quickly but I took the time to clean the barrel of my revolver, reload the empty cylinder, and made certain the hammer was in the safety notch. I was completely rearmed. I then removed six Sharps from a crate and loaded them with cartridges and caps in case we would need them, easing the hammers down so the jolting of the wagon would not set them off. Silas and Noah prepared their weapons too. We'd been in enough gun fights to make sure we were ready for the next one.

I felt exhausted. I wanted to lay down and sleep. The day had been full of risks and killing. I knew I would go over and over all of it in my mind, wondering if I could have responded differently. Did I really have to shoot the last man, as Ruth had asked? The answer would come later. I was used up, worn out, and yet, if the attack through the Ashmore farm had been a flanking movement, there might also be a battle at the sentry post. If it had already happened, maybe a small force could hit the attackers unexpectedly and save some settlers. If a battle was going on now, maybe we could repel the assault or at least slow them down. If it had not happened yet, then maybe, with the weapons and men available, we could dig in and send for reinforcements, although God alone knew how the captain would react if and when he got the message.

Silas and Noah rode horses well for infantrymen. We followed the new telegraph wires. The progress the soldiers made showed how well enlisted men could do when committed to a task and not burdened by officers. The four men had strung wire on poles and brought the ability for telegraphic communication close enough to see the outpost.

Click was standing outside, surveying the soldiers as they returned to work stringing wire.

"I just finished sending a message," he told me. "Thanks fer yer top rail number one help. We sent them varmints runnin.' I jus sent the information to Lightning Jenkins in Washington City. He'll get it to old Unconditional Surrender even if he has to kick down ev'ry door in the White House. When those chicken guts Klansmen attacked, Mica and Raymond picked off two or three Ghouls or Gizzards or whatever they're calling themselves these days. A couple others were wounded. It's gonna be hard to get the bloodstains out of some of those sheets. Word's been passed to the soldiers, but March probably don't know yet."

"So, it's quiet here now," I said, looking around.

"Yes, I reckon they skedaddled on home," said Click.

I thought for a moment. "I'll leave the telegraph crew here to finish the job and brace the poles that need support. I have Sharps and ammunition they can keep in case there's another assault. Tomorrow I'll take Raymond home and settle accounts with the captain."

"How are you gonna deal with that high muckety-muck?" he asked.

"I don't rightly know," I said. "I'll figure it out tomorrow."

I led my mules and wagon to the barn. The mules had run when I needed them to, stood steady when I used the wagon as a shooting practice, and pulled the wagon without complaint for a very long day. I unhitched them and led them into individual stalls. The water in the troughs was clean. The oats were fresh. I groomed each one and rubbed them dry with a blanket left in the barn. I talked to each of them, thanking them for the work they had done. The outlaws' horses had been fed and looked after. Silas and Noah took good care of the animals that had carried them to where they were needed.

"This barn and the house are big enough to hold a lot more than two men," I said.

"We had a different captain when they were built," said Noah. "This used to be a place we set off on patrols from. We didn't have outlaws settlin' on our land. The fences were strong where they were needed."

"He was tolerable, even if he was an officer," said Silas. "Things changed with Capt'n March."

Raymond came in and saw what we had done.

"Were you the one who mucked out the stalls and got fresh water?" I asked.

He smiled. "A good man will take care of his animals afore he takes care of himself," answered Raymond.

"True," I said. "Well, thank you for doing that. Did you clean the Sharps you used today?"

"I didn't fire many rounds. It should be fine the next time it's used," Raymond answered.

"Very likely so," I said. "Except there's no telling ahead of time how many times you'll need to shoot before you get the chance to take care of the weapon. I'd rather go into a fight knowing I have a clean weapon rather than wondering when it will be so foul that I'll lose accuracy."

"Oh. I didn't think about that," Raymond said. "What do you call your mules?"

"That's Matthew. Next to him is Mark. Third is Luke. And then comes Jenny."

CHAPTER FIVE

Sleep was hard to come by, given all the worries I had about what might happen next. Even discussing the day with my dog didn't relax me like it usually does. Darkee is a great listener. He never interrupts to express his opinion or contradict me. To distract myself, I took apart the Whitworth, admiring the workmanship and ingenuity that went into the rifle. The barrel was fouled, which happened more often than with other weapons because it was a precise piece of machinery. I cleaned the barrel thoroughly. I removed and cleaned the percussion lock firing mechanism piece by piece and lubricated the works before reassembling the weapon. Feeling I had accomplished something helped me loosen up and fall asleep.

Early the next morning I heard a call.

"Hello the sentry post. This is Abraham Harkrader. I'm here with my clan to speak with the man some call the Devil."

I shouted back, "That would be me. Give me a few minutes to get ready and I'll be out."

"His crew will be with him," yelled Mica.

We got ready, dressed, and armed ourselves.

The Harkraders' patriarch looked like Moses on horseback. His posture and bearing left no doubt that he was the leader of the dozen or so men behind him about one hundred yards from the outpost.

"I'm Ben Devlin. Speak your piece."

"Those Quaker teachers brought the bodies of four men to the church," he said. "I want to know why you killed them. They've been prowling around with some of my men."

"Did the teachers tell you that they attacked without warning while we were working on their farm?" I asked.

Harkrader's face twisted into a grimace. "They did."

"And do you believe them?" I asked.

"I do."

"Well, that's why we killed them. Getting shot at usually requires shooting back. I'll wager you would have done the same. Do you have a problem with that?"

"I ain't exactly happy about it, but I can't say I have a problem with it," said Harkrader.

"I wonder, did some o' your mob come home bloodied and needin' mending yesterday?" Mica asked. "Some Klan members showed up. We killed a few and chased off the rest of 'em. Was some of yours mixed up in that?"

Harkrader scowled and turned his head toward two men who looked away.

"Is that all the bad news?" Harkrarder's voice shook. I couldn't tell if it was from sadness or anger.

"I'm afraid not, sir," I said. "Two of your boys...."

I looked at Mica.

"Clem and Dill," he said.

"They shot at me and Raymond when we drove past," I said. "I killed them too."

Harkrader flinched. He seemed to age before my eyes.

"Sir, they and some others, maybe men in your crew, set up a place on Sherman's Shore. They have been taking potshots at the soldiers. I don't know why the captain allowed it. He has a lot to answer for."

Harkrader sat silently for what seemed like years although it could not have been longer than a few seconds.

"Damnation, those boys never had any sense. I have a lot to answer for too. How come I have to hear this now? Why didn't any of you soldiers come to me direct?"

"I tried," said Mica. "I come to your place a month ago to talk to you, but Clem and Dill told me to git afore they put me in the ground. Others in your crew seen me at your place. Ask 'em if it ain't so. The capt'n ordered me not to go back there. Musta' been one of yours told the man. I sure as hell did not."

Harkrader turned his horse around and faced his crew.

"I ain't dead yet," he announced. "Maybe you think the war hollowed me out like a tree that's already dead, but I'm still the he-coon in this outfit. Why didn't any one of you come and tell me what was going on? Mason William Harkrader, you're the oldest. Why didn't you tell me?"

"I reckoned you knew, sir," said a heavyset man on a black mare. "You spoke enough against the Yanks. You never come right out and said it, but I figured you encouraged the hot-headed boys like Dill, Clem, Alfred, and Thomas. They missed enough chores when they was off bedevilin' the coloreds. The rest of us complained, but you never said nothing to 'em."

"Damn it, you complained about them missing chores. You never said they's bothering coloreds. If'n ya'll wanna know what I think 'bout something, ask me. When did I ever say go after the coloreds? I fought the Yanks. I killed a passel of 'em whilst they was trying to kill me. I curse 'em because they killed my people and respect 'em 'cause they kept on coming. Deo vindice. I guess we know now which side God was on. I never fought 'till the bluebellies came to the South. We all risked our lives, but those men over there could have been killed or sold as slaves if they surrendered. They knew that an' fought anyway."

Harkrader paused and looked at each man in his crew individually. "Some of you are my sons by blood. Others are my sons by fighting with me in the war. No son of mine is gonna sneak around like a coward in a bed sheet with the damned Klan. None of you gonna work with the blasted lowlife captain. If you do, I swear I'll horsewhip you. You hear?"

He turned back to face me and spoke.

"Devil man, I can't say as I blame you for what you did. I'd a' done the same. But I can't let go of you killin' my sons either. I challenge you to a duel. We kin start a thousand yards apart and both shoot at the same time. If we both miss, we go to nine hundred yards and shoot again. Then eight hundred yards and so on. We use whatever weapon we have on hand. What do you say?"

Behind him, Mason William shifted his weight in the saddle.

Raymond blurted out, "That'll be the death of you, old man. I've never met anybody who could shoot as good as Ben."

"Yes, you have, Raymond," I answered. "He's sitting on that horse right in front of you. Mr. Harkrader had to be one of the top Confederate sharpshooters. Sir, I regret that I cannot accept the challenge right now. I am doing work that has to be finished soon, and I am the only one who can do it. Perhaps, if you feel the same way when my job is completed, we could discuss it then. However, I have a number of concerns about accepting your offer right now."

"You afraid?" Harkrader asked.

"Of course," I said. "You are a formidable opponent, and I want to live. If you kill me, I believe that would be the end of the dispute between me and your family. But I'm not certain that it would be over if I kill you. Your family needs a strong hand on the reins. That would be gone if you die."

"Oh, there's little chance a' me dying," he said.

"I suspect it's more likely than you think, sir," I said. "I reckon Clem and Dill had your Whitworth. I have it now."

Mason William wrenched his horse around and galloped away. Harkrader turned and stared at his son's back. Then he straightened in the saddle and faced me again.

"I'll deal with my eldest son later. You having the Whitworth only makes my challenge a more even contest," he said. "I made the challenge. I will stick by it."

"I respect that, sir, but I still have more work to do and being on the lookout for your sons would make my task harder. It would be a favor to me, sir, and I believe to your family too, if you would corral them and keep them out of my way for right now. You are the only one who has the strength to bring them to heel. And, meaning no disrespect, I'm not sure even you can control all of them. I have no wish to cause you more pain but I am determined to follow through with what I started. I cannot promise to spare their lives if they interfere."

"I lost so much in the war," said Harkrader. "Did you know that the land the sentry post is built on used to be mine? It was south of the Dickensons' land. That was taken too. More important, my wife died when I was far away. Cousins, uncles, friends, brothers in arms, two sons. The men you killed died 'cause they were still fighting that war. I cannot abide to lose anyone else. After all this is over, you and me is going to have a reckonin'."

He wheeled his horse around.

"We're going home," he announced. "We're gonna sit down and come to an understanding or some of ya'll will move on."

Then he rode away and his crew followed.

...

"Somebody else is coming," said Raymond.

"It looks like an old friend of yours," I said.

Sure enough, Dickenson and his five sons rode up from the South.

"It sure feels different when we ain't outnumbered," said Mica.

They spread out in a line and stopped about ten yards in front of us.

"If you've been looking for me, here I am," said Raymond. "I introduced myself to Mr. Devlin after ya'll left. He dint know who I was before."

"You comin' with us, boy," said Dickenson.

"No, sir," answered Raymond. "I apologize for bein' a fool and embarrassin' your young'un. I promise I won't do it again. But I'm goin' home now."

"Times have changed," said Mica. "This used to be your land, but it's ours now. We don't allow Whites to come here and hunt us down and kill us."

"I can't just turn tail," said Dickenson. "I can't show my face to my neighbors without avenging the way this boy insulted my daughter."

"It wasn't an intended insult," I said. "He didn't think. He apologized. He won't do it again. You proved your point. Go home to your family."

"I can't. Do you know what they're gonna carve on my tombstone? 'He lost the land that his family held for a hundred years.'"

"You lost it to the war," I said. "Many people lost a lot more."

"What do you know about it?" Dickenson demanded.

"I lost everything I had and everybody I knew," I answered. "They're gone forever. You still have a family. Leave before you lose that too."

"I told you, I can't!"

"Do you know what else they could put on your grave?" I asked. "They could carve 'And besides that he got his sons killed and ended his family line.' Is that how you want to be remembered?"

Dickenson glanced left and right at his sons.

"If you favor one of your sons, or more than one, send them away, sir," I said. "When the shooting starts any family member here with you will die. I know you don't fear death. Do you fear the deaths of your sons or the death of your family line?"

Dickenson sat silently.

"Do you have the courage to keep on living?" I asked. "What will happen to your daughter after her father and her brothers are all gone?"

He turned his horse and slowly rode off. His sons followed.

"Come on, Raymond," I said. "Let's get you home before you get me in any more trouble."

We set off. When an elderly man hoeing in his garden saw us, he walked toward the road.

"Raymond, who's your friend?" he asked.

"This here is Ben Devlin," answered Raymond. "He used to work for Mister Abraham Lincoln hisself. He saved my life, couple of times. Shot up a herd of Klansmen and he's on his way to straighten out the capt'n."

The man looked at me. "Is that so?"

"Some of it, if you boil down to the meat of the matter," I said. "I had the honor of working for Father Abraham. No better man ever lived. I suppose I am guilty of keeping this young rooster alive. But I can't stop him from crowing. I take no pleasure in killing, but it was necessary. As to the captain, I do have questions for the man."

"You know President Lincoln personally?"

"I do," I said.

"Will you tell him that Jonas Spellman is praying for him?" he asked.

"Jonas Spellman. I will, Mr. Spellman."

"He don't know me, of course. I never met the man, but I feel like I know him. Is that strange?"

"No, sir. Many people have told me the same. I believe he will be pleased to hear from you."

"I been praying for him. I could pray for you too."

"I would be grateful," I said. "I have a feeling I will need all the help I can get."

Each time we saw someone, Raymond would stop and introduce me. Pretty soon it got so people would be waiting for us before we got to them. News travelled faster than we could. Farms were well-kept and tidy. People dressed neatly and carried themselves with pride, however humble their estate was. I could not tell how the future would be for these people, but it would be better than the future I came from, if I could do anything about it. In my time, tenant farming was not a great deal better than slavery.

"That's my place up ahead," said Raymond. The buildings on his property were well-constructed. A neat house sat close to a sturdy barn. Even the chicken coop looked solid. A large garden next to the house included flowers as well as vegetables. The arrangement took advantage of natural elements and evoked a sense of well-being.

"You've done very well," I said.

"Thanks. Lilly is mostly responsible for how good it looks," said the young man. "She has the brains to figure out how somethin' will end up before even startin' it. The flowers an' pretties were her ideas. I don't know where she is. If she was nearby, she'd have greeted us by now."

"I'll put the mules in the barn," I said. I saw to it that they had food and water, checked their legs and hooves, and toweled them down before leaving the barn. When I stepped outside, I noticed two unusual and colorful quilts hanging out to dry. I walked over to look more closely.

"Why are you looking at my quilts?" came a woman's voice from behind me. "Most men don't pay much attention to women's work."

"I'm looking because I've never seen anything like these," I answered. "The designs in this one look like they're moving. They're like ocean waves or maybe autumn leaves blowing in the wind. The other one looks like little boxes are sticking up out of the quilt. They're remarkable, lovely. My mother was a quilter, along with her sisters. I learned enough to admire fine work."

I turned to see her and was struck almost speechless. She was the most beautiful woman I had ever seen anywhere in this time or in the times I came from. Her skin had a golden tinge to it. Her features were like those on a China doll. I closed my mouth before I started drooling like a baby. Luckily, she was looking more at the quilts than at me, which gave me time to compose myself.

"That's just a trick of mine," she said. "I'm Lilly, by the way."

"I'm Ben," I answered. "I disagree. As I said, I've never seen quilts like these. It's not easy to fool the eye. You had to be precise with cutting the angles repeatedly and arranging them. Did you have a pattern?"

"I made the patterns for both," she said. "I got some ideas from patterns I'd seen. I changed them to get the effect I wanted. Why do you ask?"

"Because I'm impressed," I answered. "If you ever get a chance to try painting, I would wager you could create beautiful things. You are an artist."

"That's total bosh," she said.

"No. I'm thinking of all the elements that went into those quilts. Please excuse me using for shooting as a comparison to your skill. Lots of men are good shots but the best marksmen treat shooting like a science. When shooting at a man riding a horse, they take the time to plan. They don't shoot at him. They shoot at where he will be when the bullet arrives. They figure out the distance, wind speed and direction, the motion of riding the horse. A bullet will drop toward the ground. Wind can alter its path. At long distances, breathing and heartbeat also matter. I respect anyone who can figure out all the elements of a complex activity. Mrs. Ashmore told me you were intelligent. This proves it."

"You are not at all what I expected," she said. "Raymond told me you kill men at the drop of a hat and that you ordered him around like he was an idiot. Those are my words, mind you, not Raymond's. He has a serious case of hero worship. He said the soldiers admire

43

you like you are a god. He talked like you were ten feet tall and stronger than an ox."

"Well, I am standing below you on the slope," I said. "That makes me look shorter than I really am. Raymond's definitely seen me act dumber than an ox. I had the privilege to serve Mr. Lincoln. No doubt some of the respect he deserves gets rubbed off him and sticks to me."

"Where in the world are you from?" asked Lilly. "Men always think what women do is simple. Very few even consider what it takes to do women's work. You don't look, think, or talk like any colored person I've ever known. I know all about presenting an image to the world so you can hide behind it. I've had to do exactly that to raise my estate in the world. You are very good at presenting what you want people to think you are. People almost never look beyond their expectations. Why are you pretending to be something you are not? And what exactly are you?"

"I am from a place so far away that I'll never be able to return to it. I am just a man making the best of a situation I cannot change. I am determined to do what I can to make this time and place better until my efforts get me killed. That's why I protected President Lincoln. That's why I am here now."

"Almost nobody understands how hard it is to stay in character when you are in a play that never ends," said Lilly. "You cannot afford to be yourself. After playing a part for a long time, you don't really know any more who you are."

She put her hand on my arm. "You and I are alike. We are trapped in a world where we don't belong. With each other, we can let our guard down. You don't have to continue fighting until you die. We could leave this life, this place. In New York or Philadelphia, we could reinvent ourselves. We could say we're from another part of the world. Nobody could prove we aren't. I could please you any way you like."

"It's tempting," I said. "You are an intriguing woman. Maybe if we had met some other place or some other time, it might have been possible."

"You know my history," she said. "You talked to Mrs. Ashmore. You really mean if so many men had not had me before you."

44

"No, I don't. You aren't to blame for what happened to you," I told her. "That was totally out of your control. What I mean is that I can't abandon these people here when they've been set up for slaughter. I don't know the exact plan, but Captain March is up to his eyebrows in it. I have to confront him and stop it."

Lilly smiled. "I can tell you," she said. "He hates coloreds. He plan to let the KKK to attack while he sends out the soldiers into small groups. The Klan will attack a patrol setting up a telegraph wire. A second group will take over the sentry post. Then they'll combine forces and outnumber the rest. When they finish them off, they'll burn down the farms and kill as many people in this place as they can. Captain March will resign from the Army in disgrace and then disappear. He'll send a suicide note to his wife and children and never be seen again."

I felt a chill down my spine. March's plan was close to what I had suspected. My heart pounded.

"How do you know the plan in such detail?" I asked.

The smile on her face vanished.

"Capt'n told me."

"Why?" I asked.

Her eyes flitted from side to side.

"Let me guess," I said. "He is going to disappear. With you. But you know you could never trust a man who hates coloreds as much as he does. He will betray you sooner or later. Once the two of you show up far away and you get identified as his wife, you will find a way to get rid of him or, maybe more likely, get somebody to do it for you."

"Kin you blame me?" she hissed.

"Actually, no," I said. "You'd be defending yourself. He deserves it. And I don't blame you for whatever you did with the men who abused you, either. But you sent Raymond into town in a hey-look-at-me shirt, knowing he was so puffed up and prideful that he was going to act like a banty rooster and might get himself killed. You could just disappear without getting him harmed. And now you are involved with a man who plans for the murders of the soldiers and settlers here. There are other ways to escape besides with him, Lilly. You could find a place where you are not known and easily ac-

45

quire a white husband there who would not abuse you."

"You wrong 'bout things," she said. "And none of them terrible things happened yet."

"Not yet. I'm going to make sure they don't."

"Raymond will never believe you," she said.

"He might. It doesn't matter." My heart ached. "Lilly, you would do well to leave him and this place far behind you. You ought to consider some place out west. Someone might recognize you in an eastern city. Los Angeles or San Francisco would be a good place to start over. Nobody asks too many questions in those places."

"Let me 'splain," she said. "Don't hate me."

"I don't have time to listen right now. I don't like some of the choices you made, but I certainly do not hate you. Thank you for telling me the captain's plan. With all my heart, I wish you well. I truly hope you can escape the bitter past."

I ran to the barn to get my wagon and my mules, wiped tears out of my eyes, and started off to stop a massacre.

Before I got to headquarters, I met Lieutenant Reynolds leading a patrol. I showed him my letter from the president and outlined the situation.

"Unfortunately, I don't know the time of the raid or the number of raiders," I said.

"If they've already probed the defenses, it has to be soon," said the officer. "What are your orders?"

"Send two men on fast horses to the closest homesteads. Tell the settlers to spread the word to others to get their weapons out of the armory and get ready to defend their homes. Contact Franks and tell him to reinforce the Ashmore farm and the sentry post. You do the same. I suggest a fishhook formation by the sentry post, leaving a few men to guard against an approach from the sea. I think their scouts will say there were a few men by the post with good weapons. Based on that, they might charge the post, planning to take casualties to overwhelm it. If they do, I suggest having a few men return fire. Others should stay under cover. Once the whole force is engaged, I'd have the rest of the men in front of them open fire. After that, men all along their flank — the shaft of the hook — should join in. Warn the men to wait their turn."

"That would make a deadly killing ground," said Reynolds.

"We are not interested in taking prisoners," I said. "They're coming to slaughter women and children. It's all guesswork. No plan survives the reality of battle. I trust you to alter the plan after you see what really happens."

"Won't you come with us?" asked Reynolds. "The men have been talking up your shooting skill. By this time the captain likely knows something is up. Some of the soldiers at the fort are going to support him no matter what. You'll be safer if you wait until after the upcoming fight so we can arrive in force."

I shrugged. "Unfortunately, we don't have an idea about when the attack will come. I don't want Captain March to slip away unannounced. And I don't have absolute proof he is behind the whole enterprise. I want to hear his explanation directly. Let's unload the weapons and bullets from my wagon to your cart so you can be on your way. I will get the guard away from the armory. I promise to do my best to stay alive until you get back."

CHAPTER SIX

As I approached the gate to the fort, I noticed that each side of the gate was pegged into the ground. Just inside, a guard I did not know stepped in front of the mules. I pulled the reins and the mules stopped.

"Did you see anyone headed this way while you came to camp?" the sergeant demanded.

"Just some soldiers," I answered. "They were some distance off." They had been only a foot or so away. He didn't ask for more information and I didn't offer any. "Are you expecting someone?"

He turned his head and spat.

"Yeah. Some bigwig from Washington City's on the way to tell the captain everything he's doin' wrong. I don't know the bastard or even his name, but I figure he'll be driving a fancy buggy or half-falling off an old plow horse."

"I suppose he could have a driver," I said.

The soldier chuckled. "Could be some perfumed, pampered former house slave up there with one of them parasols is driving, ready to do him any favor he wants."

He waved me on.

The dog sat on the wagon seat beside me as we rode up the street. I rubbed him on the head and said, "I've never seen a fort like this one. The front gate is wide open and tethered. It doesn't make sense. They'd never be able to close the gate in time if they were attacked."

As we rolled on slowly, I continued my commentary.

"Look there. Most forts just have visitors put their animals in the Army corral, but that's a separate livery. Wilber's Livery. Right next to it is Wilber's Emporium and General Store. Across the street is Wilber's Saloon and then Wilber's Hotel."

The dog listened with interest but had no reaction. I reached over and patted him. A young copper-skinned woman wearing a tattered robe launched herself from the sidewalk in front of the hotel and wobbled into the street. She swayed toward starboard and overcorrected toward port before she lost her balance entirely and capsized into the mud. Luckily, traffic was light. I stopped the wagon and walked over to her.

"You all right, miss?" I asked.

She mumbled something but made no effort to stand.

"Did you come from the hotel?" I asked. Up close the odor of whiskey about her was strong. She was not wearing anything under her robe. I didn't want her to get run over so I lifted her out of the mire and carried her into the hotel. Nobody was at the front desk. I deposited her gently in an armchair. I picked up a handbell on the desk and rang it. An older man limped into the room.

"Why'd you go and dump her on a clean chair?" he asked.

"I thought somebody would drive right over her. I suppose I could have dropped her on your desk."

"Toby, stop," came a female voice. A woman came down the stairs. She looked at me. "Where did you find Rosita?" She walked toward the young woman in the chair.

She was a heavyset woman, with more makeup plastered on her face than I had seen on any other woman. Her hair was straightened and arranged stylishly. She wore a long, colorful robe. Her legs showed as she walked.

"She fell down in the street in front of me," I said. "I believe she's drunk."

Toby snorted and left the room.

"She should be asleep. She'll be workin' all night long." The woman smiled at me. "Thanks for bringin' her home, I'm Bonnie," she said. She struck a pose to show off her impressive bosom.

She was trying so hard to be seductive that I decided not responding would hurt her feelings.

"You certainly are," I said. "Sorry, I bet you hear that a lot. I'm Ben."

"I don't hear it nearly as much as I used to, Ben," she said. "It's rare to find a gentleman in these parts. Ya' got covered in mud, looking out for Rosita. I'd like to offer a room, a bath, an' to clean your clothes for free."

"Thank you, Bonnie," I said. "I wonder if you wouldn't mind sharing some conversation too. Just conversation."

"I'd be delighted, sir."

"My wagon is blocking the street at the moment," I said. "Let me get my mules taken care of, and I'll take advantage of your kindness."

I drove to the livery. A youngster named Ted showed me where I could stable the mules.

"Them are good-lookin' animals," he said. "You could sell them and make good money. Sherman didn't have enough Army surplus mules to sell to everybody. Do you mind if I take a closer look?"

"Not at all, Ted," I said. "They're good-tempered. Just let them know you're coming."

He inspected Matthew. "They've been well-cared for. Old man Wilber would give you top dollar."

"Is he the man who's got his name on everything I see here?" I asked.

"Plus, other businesses like the bank that's on another street. He owns everything the Army don't. Him and the captain are partners, I reckon. You'll know him if you see him. He'll be the only white man 'round here not wearing a uniform. You'll know his man Hosea if you see a man bigger than a grizzly bear wearing a derby. He does what Wilber tells him to do."

When I returned to the hotel with my belongings, Toby glared at me, but he checked me in. I had not had a hot bath for quite some time. It was wonderful. I cleared my mind and relaxed, knowing the peace would not last. I checked my revolvers and put them in a double holster. I carried a fully loaded replacement cylinder. When I appeared in the lobby wearing clean clothes, Bonnie was waiting for me. Toby scowled.

"Don't let him bother you," said Bonnie. "He has the great misfortune of being in love with me 'spite all the heartache that causes. Any time I show interest in a man, he grouses like a spoiled child."

"It ain't fair," said Toby. "I bet you got schoolin,' been places I ain't even heard of. She don't pay no attention to me no more. I'm like an old pair of shoes."

"Shoes get more comfortable the older they get," I said to Toby. "Besides, you'll still be here when I am long gone. I'm a passing fancy. Nothing more. I won't take her away from you. I don't know that I could."

Toby mumbled and shook his head but ignored us after that.

"Your other clothes have been washed and are hanging on a line to dry," said Bonnie. You're a kindly man. Most would taunt poor old Toby or make fun of him. I'm guessing you've had some losses in your life what help you feel what others feel. Was it in the war?"

I sighed. "Yes," I said. "I lost everything I had and everyone I knew. They're gone forever. Mind, I'm not complaining. Many gave their lives. I came through without a scratch. I think nearly everybody lost someone."

I sighed again. For some reason I felt that Bonnie was someone I could talk with openly. I Imagined she had already heard nearly everything that could be said. "Maybe the worst for me is what I became. I'd never killed a man before the war. Now, I can't say how many times I've dealt out death."

She nodded. I thought I saw tears forming in her eyes.

"I'm part Romani," she said. "Can I look at your hands so I can tell your future?"

I turned my palms upward and she took them in her hands and looked at them intently.

"You have calluses in interesting places," she said. "You don't sit in an office all day. You work but not with farm tools or in a factory. You carried your baggage up the stairs like it was light as air. You are stronger than you look. I'd guess you are plenty quick too. You ain't no braggart. Quite the opposite."

"I don't know what being Romani has to do with being observant and smart," I said.

"We use all the gifts we has," she answered. "Jest like you. I can

51

usually read more about men than I can with you. Don't know where you're from. Most'd think you colored but with that hair and face, you are from somewhere far, far away."

"Really far away," I said. "You'd think I was crazy if I told you where. It's somewhere I'll never be able to return to."

She traced one of the lines with her fingertip and said, "You have the hands of a pistolero, but they have dead eyes. You don't. If I had to guess, I'd say you was a lawman on a mission."

"Close enough," I said. "I need to know what's going on here."

"This place needs to be taken out and shook like a dusty rug left on the floor too long," Bonnie said. "Old man Wilber, he own it all, lock, stock an' barrel. He can't legally own the land. The captain claims the Army owns the space inside an' 'round the fort. He allows Wilber to operate but nobody else. March must be getting a heap of money from him. Now, I admit there are some 'vantages to soldiers. It's safe to get pie-eyed drunk. When they lonely, they can find my girls close to home. They won't get beat or killed if they pass out. Keeping all us coloreds away from Whites keeps trouble from happening."

"But keeping the groups separated also means the Whites never have to accept us or learn who we are as individuals," I said.

"And all the soldiers' pay goes straight to a man who is used to making his livin' off the sweat of the Black race," said the madam.

"I'm most concerned about the safety of the people who live here," I said. "March let marauders set up close to the southern entrance where they could outnumber and outgun the sentries, who have no way to communicate to the fort. He allowed a break in the border fence where enemies could pour through in strength. Here the gate is staked wide open. Attackers can roll over the sentries from two directions, combine forces, burn through the homesteads, and overwhelm the garrison before anyone knows they're here. It's a massacre waiting to happen."

"I know," said Bonnie. "We been low-hanging fruit for months. But what can we do about it? Besides run? And where would we go? For how long?"

Toby spoke up. "I'm loaded for bear behind the front desk, but I can't be here every second of every day."

"I don't know when it will come," I said. "The attack might not get this far. However, it is coming and I think it will be soon. Toby, I suggest you fortify the desk, double the supply of whatever weapons you keep there and always carry a revolver with you. Bonnie, surely some of your girls know how to shoot. I'd warn them and arm them."

"How do you know?" asked Bonnie.

"Well, I've been poking at the hornets' nest," I said. "Part of the reason I'm here is to get the arsenal unlocked so the settlers can defend themselves. Where is the arsenal?"

"It's up the next street to the left," said Toby. "Right next door to headquarters. Soon as you do anythin', the capt'n will know."

"Good, he and I need to have a conversation," I said. "Stay safe."

I walked to the arsenal. The same soldier I met when I entered the post was standing with his arms crossed over his chest, facing an angry group of men.

"I told you, I ain't openin' the door," he said to the crowd. " Capt'n March ordered me to keep it locked."

He glared at me. I took out the letter from President Grant and handed it to him. He read it painfully slowly. I waited without saying a word.

"You the bigwig I was waiting for," he announced. "You coulda told me."

"I suppose I could have, but I wanted to look around on my own. My order to you is to unlock the door and let these men get their weapons."

"How do I know they won't take guns that belong to the Army?"

"They look like an honest bunch," I answered. I turned toward the men. "The door will be unlocked directly. I expect you to behave in an orderly manner. Go in one at a time and take only what belongs to you and leave quickly so the next man gets his turn. Go fast. The sergeant will remain to see that there are no problems."

"I don't expect 'em to only take their own weapons," said the soldier.

"Well, Sarge, if any man tries to take a cannon, stop him. Otherwise, don't interfere."

I walked to the headquarters building and entered. An overweight corporal sat in a chair in the waiting room. A map of the area hung on one wall. The closed door of what I presumed was an office hung on the wall behind the desk where a short, skinny private sat.

"Whoa," said the fat man. "Here I was just sayin' to Paul that somethin' is in the air, and lo and behold, in walks the devil to prove it."

"Hello, Billy Bob," I said. "Is Captain March in?"

The private looked at me and raised his eyebrows as if asking a question. "He's in his office an' he don' wanna be bothered."

"Good. I won't bother him right now," I said. "Right now, I need the two of you to read this letter." I handed the letter from the President to Paul. Billy Bob lumbered over to the desk. Paul scanned it quickly, while Billy Bob watched him. I doubted that Billy Bob could read.

"My goodness," said Paul. "You represent the president and outrank the captain?"

"That's it," I said. "Now, I need the two of you to explain that to every soldier you see and tell them to pass it on. Tell them my orders are like orders from the President himself. It does not matter what the captain says or does. I am in complete command. Understand?"

"Yes, sir," said Paul.

"You two get to it. I will deal with the captain."

54

CHAPTER SEVEN

I sat in a chair and tipped it back to rest against the wall. There was little to gain by facing the captain before the soldiers spread the news about their new commander. I still did not know when the attack would start, but I did not want complications that could come from soldiers obeying orders from the captain rather than from me. After about ten minutes the sergeant who had been at the armory came through the door to the outside.

"Do you intend to tell the captain that I'm now in charge?" I asked.

He nodded.

"I'll come with you," I said.

The sergeant knocked on the office door. Nothing happened. He knocked again, louder this time.

"What do you want?" demanded a voice from inside the office.

"Sir, I really need to talk with you," said the soldier.

"What about?"

"Sir, it would be easier to explain to you in person."

I held up the letter.

"Sir, there's someone and something you need to see for yourself."

"Awright, damn it, but make it quick."

Captain March sat behind a desk situated on a raised platform. It gave him a height advantage over anyone sitting in the other chairs in the room. He rose to his feet, which I noticed put him eye to eye with the enlisted man. I was shorter than both of them.

"What the hell is so important?" In a room full of army officers, he would not have warranted a second glance. His thinning brown hair was plastered down to cover as much bald pink flesh as possible, and his eyes were the color of shadows.

I stepped forward and laid the open letter on his desk. He picked it up and started reading. His eyes widened. The longer he read, the redder his complexion became. Trembling, he threw the paper down.

"I suppose you think this puts you in command?"

"Yes, sir, I believe you're correct," I said. "I am now in charge."

"Sergeant, you may leave," said March.

"No, Sergeant, stay," I said.

The man flinched but remained in the room.

"I had no idea you were colored, boy," said the officer. "You're the one the soldiers call the devil. I cannot imagine why. I heard a rumor that you'd been ambushed and killed. They said you had been replaced by a spy using your name. I put out an order to watch out for that."

"That is odd," I said. "I wonder how someone figured out both my name and my mission. I didn't find out about it until it was assigned to me. Through the end of the war, Confederate intelligence gathering was getting worse. I was just one of many men protecting the President. I can't imagine I attracted much attention from the rebs. Where did you hear the rumor and from whom?"

"I don't recall exactly," said March. "I think I heard bits and pieces at different times from different people. Now that the war is over, they're getting really careless in Washington City."

"Can I talk to some of the people who mentioned something about it?"

"Sorry, the only person I'm sure I heard it from has moved to the Oregon territory," he said. "The mistake had to be made within the government. Many people tell me they don't like the way coloreds are stepping out of line. They blame them for the war."

"I wonder," I answered.

"Say, Ben," he started. "I hope you don't mind that I do not call you Mr. Devlin. I never got used to the idea of addressing someone of the Black race as 'mister' or 'doctor' or whatever ridiculous title they claim to have."

"Oh, that's not a problem, Jimmy," I answered.

The captain gritted his teeth and shook his head.

"Oh, you don't want to be on a first-name basis?" I asked. "Very well. I don't have a military rank. And you would prefer not to call me Mr. Devlin. Hmm, I know. I'll call you Captain. You can either call me Mr. Devlin or you can call me Sir. Which would you prefer?"

He looked like he might have vomited in his throat. He nodded. "Can Sergeant Mills be dismissed....Mr. Devlin?"

"I prefer that he stay," I said. "I often find that a person not involved in a conversation has a better memory about it than either of those who were talking."

"Can we walk around the fort as we talk?" asked March.

"That's a good idea. Let's take a walk and you can answer my questions. Mills, come with us, and let every soldier we pass know about the change in the command structure."

"Yes, sir," said Mills.

The captain hesitated before he stepped from behind his desk, but after a moment, he did. When he stepped off the platform, I determined that he was about my height. We went outside.

I started the conversation with a compliment. "The surrounding fortifications are impressive. The main gate looks sturdy. Maybe you can explain why the gate to the inner area is wide open and staked to stay that way."

"Well, unlike every other settlement of coloreds, we have never had any serious conflict here with people."

"By people do you mean White people?" I asked.

"Exactly. With real people," said the officer. "So, there's no need to be able to fortify this place."

"Does that mean there never will be?" I asked. "Do you know that for certain for all time?"

"Of course, I cannot say what will happen when others take command," he said. "I just know there is no need while I am here."

"And why is that?"

"You coloreds don't know how to get along with people," he said. "I understand them. I treat them like small children. I tell them what to do, how to do it, and when to do it. But mostly I keep them away from people who don't understand that they're not like us. When something goes wrong, I punish the coloreds, even if it's not strictly their fault. I want to teach them to avoid people, and that way we avoid problems."

"Interesting," I said.

"It is unlikely in the extreme that this place will be besieged by a large force equipped with cannons and war material," he said.

"Yes," I said. "Other settlements have only faced raiders on horseback and disorganized mobs. In those cases, having a way to hold the invaders at bay and having time to organize a defense under cover have saved a lot of lives. I don't see how that would be possible here with the gates immobile. Do you?"

"That's a highly unlikely event, but, if you wish, I will have the gates unblocked," said March.

"Mills," I said to the soldier, "what is that squad of men over there doing?"

"I believe they have been ordered to dig new latrines, sir."

"Tell whoever is in charge of the group that they are reassigned to unblock the gates, grease the hinges or otherwise get the gates to swinging freely, locate the cross bar and practice closing and barring the gates until it goes as smoothly as clockwork and quickly as a second hand. We will wait for you here while you give the instructions."

While we waited in silence, the captain avoided looking me in the eye. When the soldier returned, I started walking again.

"Of course, one of the ways casualties were minimized when other settlements were attacked was by quick and accurate communication," I said to March. "Would you care to tell me why you have not finished the telegraph line between here and the southern sentry outpost?"

A few soldiers approached us and began to shadow our movements.

"How do you know…?" he asked. "It is not necessary, in my opinion. I know the townspeople and the soldiers. I thought other matters were more urgent."

"You thought putting the line through to Springfield was more important than completing it to the outpost? Really?" I asked. "Please explain your reasoning."

More soldiers, noticing the odd group, joined our listeners.

Beads of sweat formed on the officer's forehead. "Um, again the peace between the coloreds and the people. It would help relations with the town." His voice trailed off.

"Perhaps it is because I did not ever get military training that your answer makes absolutely no sense to me at all," I said. "Mills, do you understand?"

"No, sir," said Mills.

"Captain, please expand on your answer. I have been told that your primary goal is to protect the settlers. How does something that leaves a gap in defenses in favor of benefitting people you are not ordered to cover as part of your instructions advance the safety of residents here?"

Other military men fell in with the growing group.

"Well, put that way, I should perhaps change my decision," he said.

"Maybe," I said. "I am also puzzled that you assigned only two men to guard duty there. How can two men stop an incursion by even a small force?"

March did not answer. His head swung from side to side so he could look at the men crowded around us.

"In my untutored experience, two men would be killed quickly, even if they had a means to ask for reinforcements, which they don't. What am I missing, sir?"

"Very," March started and stopped. "Unlikely."

"Really?" I asked. "Haven't outlaws already firmly established themselves in a building that stood there on government land for months? Do you think that discourages the thought that it would be easy to attack? Or does it encourage such ideas? I am very interested in your assessment of the situation. You see, in other areas of Sherman's Shore, the officers have behaved quite differently. I have heard them express the opinion that a well-fortified position where a number of soldiers can be seen sends the message 'hands off'."

"That— That might be seen as provocative," March said.

I stopped. Men now surrounded us, standing silently.

"You believe that demonstrating the willingness to defend yourself and your family is provocative?" I asked. "I think it shows that you're solidly planted on land you own, bought by blood and sacrifice. I think it shows that you will not be moved."

He was silent.

"Captain, I require a comprehensive written explanation of every instance where you neglected the defense of the people you were commanded to protect, including the situations I mentioned plus the gap in the fence on the land that you allow the Quakers to farm on, and all the rest too."

"I will return to my office and begin to explain."

"No, you will not," I said. "That office is no longer yours. I'm certain will you find paper and ink in the officers' quarters. You are ordered to stay away from what is now my office. I will return to what is now my office and examine whatever I find there to help me understand what you have been up to."

"This is outrageous!" said March. "I will do no such thing."

"Very well." I looked at the men standing around us. "Your former commanding officer is hereby relieved of command, according to the power granted me by President Ulysses S. Grant. Some of you know Unconditional Surrender Grant personally. You know how quickly he becomes displeased when his orders are not followed. Let me be perfectly clear: I am now in charge."

Someone in the crowd started singing and soon The Battle Cry of Freedom rang out. Men cheered and called out my name.

March's eyes widened and then he dropped his glance to the ground.

I let the noise swell for a few minutes and then waved my arms to quiet the throng. "Obviously we need to organize a band to drown out the off-key singing."

They laughed.

"March, you can either go to the officers' quarters and start writing or I will find someone to escort you to a locked cell."

Several men immediately volunteered. March walked toward the officers' quarters quietly. Mills walked with him.

CHAPTER EIGHT

I must have sensed movement from high on my right side when I opened the headquarters outside door and stepped through. I moved my head to the right and purposely fell in that direction. Even so, a vicious blow sent me crashing to the floor. Pain erupted on the left side of my head. I hit the floor and skidded. While the pain turned from massive and undifferentiated to throbbing, I felt my revolvers being yanked from my holsters. The world was gradually coming back into focus.

I heard a voice, deep and rumbling, ask, "How come he ain't 'sleep?"

"I dint hit him wid my skull-cracker. Dint want to kill him, but any mortal man be out like a snuffed-out candle. His eyes still open."

Another voice answered, "They call him Devil. Help me carry him into the office and set him in the desk chair."

I felt myself being lifted by the back of my shirt and my belt. Someone slid me, surprisingly gently, into the desk chair. My head, or whatever was left of it, rested on my chest. I didn't have the strength to raise it. I heard a sound. After a few seconds, I identified the sound as the door to the outer room being locked. My thinking was slow. I figured out two men had struck me on the head. They took my weapons. They carried me into the inner office and placed me in the chair behind the desk. Something under the desktop looked familiar. No wonder March had wanted Mills to leave the office.

That bastard.

The elephant dancing on my head slowed up slightly. I could have raised my head, but I waited until I could string one thought after another. My vision cleared somewhat. It occurred to me that I couldn't hear the two men talking. No bragging or idle chatter. Whoever they were, they had worked together long enough that they had no need. I gingerly brought my head up.

"What." I sounded hoarse. "What did you hit me with? The butt of a pistol?"

"My fist an' my knuckle duster."

I recognized the deep voice I'd heard earlier.

"How come you kin talk an' make sense?" he asked. "You should be 'sleep for days. I must be gettin' soft an' old."

"I must be getting old and sloppy," I said. "I didn't even consider checking the office for an ambush." A muscular man with skin the color of mahogany, wearing a derby hat, sat in a chair in front of the desk. A white-haired smooth-shaven white man sat in another chair. My thoughts sluggishly knit together.

"Hosea and…Wilber," I said. "I heard about you two. Like a fool I thought I could deal with you later."

"You were mistaken," said Wilber. "I understand. You had a lot on your mind. There's no reason to apologize. We can talk now."

I blinked. "My head feels like a draft horse stomped on it," I said.

"No doubt," said Wilber. "Now, you should know that I don't care about Whites versus coloreds. I used to be a slave trader, but the only colors I care about now are silver and gold. How does March's fall affect my businesses? You are the new commander. Congratulations. Keeping in mind that we could have killed you and we didn't, what terms are you interested in to keep my businesses operating? March did very well for himself. He always took payments in gold or silver and squirreled them away in some hiding place."

"Ouch," I said. "Give me a minute." I took a couple of breaths. "Wilber, you grabbed the wrong end of a rattlesnake. How much attention have you been paying to conditions in Beulah Land?"

"I pay attention to my business in and around the fort," he said. "The rest is not my concern."

"You have been as foolish to ignore the rest as I was to ignore you," I said. "March plans to have the Klan make what Sherman did in Georgia look like a Sunday School picnic. He wants them to kill the soldiers, murder the settlers, and burn everything to the ground. He's made at least three attempts to assassinate me. I suspect he plans to destroy every clue to his involvement and disappear. He surely has plans to dispose of you two."

Wilber's eyes narrowed.

"Even if you survive, this place will be crawling with federal lawmen looking for somebody to blame for the massacre. I work for President Grant. When he goes after someone or something, he doesn't stop until he gets it."

"My, my, I knew March was scum," Wilber said. "I knew he hated coloreds. I did not know he was willing to order murder on a grand scale. A lot of pieces of the puzzle just fell in place. It's a good thing I saved your life."

It took me a moment to figure out what he meant.

"You saved my life … from you," I said.

"Exactly. We have common goals. For the moment we can put aside how much I will pay you for working for me. You are in my debt."

"I don't think so. I am saving your life right now. We are even. I don't work for you."

Wilber smiled. "Maybe that clout on the head left you unable to think clearly."

"No. We both made the same mistake thinking about March. He is more dangerous than he appears. The outer wall of this desk is a thin piece of wood. He installed a sawed-off double-barrel shotgun on a swivel under the desktop."

Wilber whistled.

"Partners then," said Wilber, "like I am with Hosea."

"For the moment only," I said. "When the troubles end, I am still the man in charge of the fort. You are the man who built buildings on land you have no claim to."

I closed my eyes and slumped forward.

"Wait," said Hosea. "You da man who saved Father Abraham from John Wilkes Booth?"

"No, I'm the man who delayed Booth by being his punching bag until colored troops piled on him. He would have gotten away if I'd been the only one fighting him."

Hosea nodded. "I seein' if you tell da truth. You is. I'm sorry I hit you so hard. If'n I knew you was you, I wouldn't have."

"It's not your fault. I'm the fool who waltzed through the door without thinking."

I tried to stand, but I had to grab the desk to keep from falling.

"This place is as ready for trouble as it can be," I said. "You keep an eye on the captain. I'll get a fast horse and join the men to the south."

"No," said Hosea. "You fall off da horse and hit your head, you die."

"We'll take you to the hotel," said Wilber. "You need to sleep."

They ignored my protests and struggles, dragging me to the hotel and up into my room. They laid me on the bed. Bonnie entered.

"Bonnie, I have to get to my men at the borders." I tried to lift myself up, and the walls in the room swayed. I lay my head back on the pillow.

"Hush," she said. "You not in shape to do anythin'."

"Bonnie, my head aches. My mind won't stop thinking of everything that could go wrong. How can I possibly sleep?"

"Leave that to me," she said. "I know exactly what to do. I have a tea that makes people drowsy. We'll pull the curtains and keep it quiet. Rest. I'll bring water and food. You have to let your body recover."

...

When I woke up, I was not sure where I was. Then I saw Toby sitting in a chair with a shotgun across his lap.

"About time you woke up, Sleeping Beauty," Toby said. "Ev'rybody but you been working fer the past week." He gestured to the weapon on his lap. "This ain't for you. Hosea an' old man Wilber took off once the other soldiers arrived to guard the fort. They made me swear to keep you safe till they got back."

"What? What other soldiers? Where'd they go? What's going

on?"

"You must be feelin' better. You back to bein' a pest again," he said, stepping toward the door. "Looie Franks, get in here. He finally woke up."

I was able to sit up. When Franks entered, he asked, "How are you feeling?"

I realized the pain was mostly gone. I could see clearly. My thoughts were orderly.

"I'm much better, thank you. Surprisingly well for having been in bed so long," I said.

"You can thank Bonnie for that," said Franks. "She had you up and walking the day after you got hurt. She insisted that you keep moving as much as you could without hurting yourself. She had you carrying heavy furniture."

"I sort of remember that," I said.

"She said that keeping your body in working condition would help you recover. Physically, you seem nearly as healthy as before your bell got rung. She nursed a lot of soldiers during the war. Patients that did what she told them to do did well."

"Please tell me what's been going on," I said. "Start at the beginning and go slowly. I have a vague memory that you've told me about things, but it's fuzzy."

Franks gathered his thoughts. "Well, let's see. Where to start? Colored troops from Fort William Carney arrived to take over defense of Fort Delany a few days after you got ambushed. They said President Grant got a telegram from you and he sent them. As soon as they showed up, old man Wilber and Hosea headed to the Ashmore farm to tell me. They stayed. That was a good thing. Reynolds and I didn't know how strong the attack would be there. We guessed wrong. I stayed with eight men. We crouched at the bottom of the makeshift wall — the fence — that the soldiers had built. Twelve Klansmen showed up."

"What happened?"

"Four horses arrived at the fence at about the same time. As I ordered, four designated soldiers shot the men in their heads. That evened the sides. The rest was a melee. Not knowing the strength of the barricade, some riders tried to force their way through. Hosea pulled at least two men off their horses and broke their necks. Wilber fired a sawed-off shotgun into a knot of men. The rest turned to flee, and the eight soldiers who still had loaded rifles fired at them. Then we used pistols. Only two of them rode away. Both were seriously injured. One fell off his horse. I hopped over the fence and ran to capture him. I bound his wounds so he would not bleed to death right then and there, helped him mount his horse, and led the horse back. They found the body of the other man not far off."

Franks bowed his head.

"By the time I returned, all the Klansmen at the farm were dead. I knew some were alive when I left. A few of them anyway. I didn't think to give an order to take them alive."

"It's not your fault," I said. "In the heat of battle men do things they would never do in other circumstances. Remember, the marauders set out to murder women and children. Besides, Hosea and Wilber were not under your command. I bet an examination of the bodies would show that a number of them died from physical injuries, not gunshot wounds. It speaks well of you as a man that the deaths bother you. For me, I have seen too many massacres of coloreds to have sympathy for the dead men. What were our casualties?"

"Three wounded, one badly. Nobody died."

"Excellent." I leaned back, tired out by talking.

"Reynolds is outside," said Franks. "Should I send him in?"

"Yes, please."

Reynolds entered and saluted me.

"We were attacked at about the same time as the others. The fishhook formation worked perfectly, sir. They didn't charge in. They rode in as quiet as rabbits. Twenty in all. They lined up and started shooting up the outpost at the same time. Put more holes in it than an acre-sized prairie dog town."

"How many of our men did they kill right then and there?"

"None, sir. Mica suggested we move all the men out ahead of time, just in case. We set up the bottom curve of the fishhook around the building. Once they emptied their weapons and the smoke cleared, our men opened fire. The Klansmen were decimated. When they turned to retreat, they had to ride along the straight line of the hook. Sharpshooters at the end of the line took down the few who got that far. Very few. Settlers who had joined us went out and dispatched the wounded. No survivors. It was like the battle of the Alamo."

"At Fort Pillow, Battle of the Crater, Poison Springs, and Saltville, colored troops were killed while trying to surrender or while being treated for wounds. None of these soldiers or settlers will ever forget. They are done forever with surrendering."

Reynolds nodded.

"Well done, Lieutenant," I said. "Luckily, you ignored my idea of where to set the hook. Also, you put the sharp shooters in the right place."

"That was Click's idea, sir."

"You were smart enough to listen to your enlisted men. What were the casualties?"

"No deaths on our side. The Klan pretty much disarmed themselves at the start. We had a few minor injuries. No settlers died."

"It sounds like Beulah Land is finally safe," I said. "So, what is it that all of you are not telling me? Why is Toby still guarding me? The Dickensons?"

"Nope," said Toby. "They done moved on to 'nother part a' the state."

"Is it my unfinished business with the Harkraders then?"

Franks glanced at Reynolds. "I left something out on my report about the battle at the Ashmore farm. I told you one attacker survived. He is Mason William Harkrader, Abraham Harkrader's oldest son."

"Well, now, that is something I need to deal with. Also, I had Harkrader's Whitworth. I gave it to Mica, who seems to have made good use of it. I told the old man we could talk after matters here were resolved. I need to send him a message."

I looked at the officers. "But Harkrader is not the kind of man to sneak up on someone. He'd come through the front door with guns blazing. So, who are you protecting me from?"

Franks and Reynolds exchanged another look.

"I told you we couldn't keep it from him," said Reynolds.

"In the confusion after the Fort Carney soldiers arrived, we lost track of Captain March," said Franks. "He tricked Sergeant Mills and escaped. Mills is deeply embarrassed and apologetic. We don't know where March went to. We're pretty sure he's not here, but he is a snake. He took over here two years ago, so he could have hidey holes anywhere."

"The marshal in Springfield is looking for him," said Reynolds. "With so many dead Klansmen, we got his attention. We've just about cleaned out the state, and lawmen are grateful."

"And impressed," added Franks. "Sherman made Georgia howl. Former slaves made Klan disappear."

"You worried that much about March?" I asked.

"Not really," said Reynolds. "We worry more about you. When Grant heard you were hurt, he burned up the telegraph wires demanding to know how you were and threatening us with what would happen if you died. We worry that you will get out of bed and bite off more than you can chew right now."

"You make twisters look lazy," said Franks. "Can you take it easy at least until you get your bearings back?"

"Thanks to you, yes, I can relax," I said. "My biggest fear did not happen. I couldn't let up because President Grant let me know before he sent me that he doesn't expect Congress to approve extending army-protection of the Sherman settlements along the coast and the islands of Georgia and South Carolina. The colonies will have to survive on their own. I can tell you now because it'll soon become public information."

"Won't the troops that are leaving tempt the White ruffians to try their luck?" asked Reynolds.

"Congress will discharge the colored troops and pay their wages due plus a bonus for cutting short their enlistments. Grant is not the politician Lincoln was, but he did arrange for the men to be offered forty acres in the settlements. White invaders will have to face the men who just destroyed the Klan. Former soldiers should just about fill up all the unclaimed land in this area. Wouldn't that make you think twice?"

Toby whistled. "Yes, sir."

"What now?" asked Franks.

"Let's see. I'd like to see Mica. Tell him to bring the Whitworth.

68

Find out how healthy Harkrader's son is, please. I still have to face his father. Where are my weapons? I have a lot of target practice to catch up on."

CHAPTER NINE

A week later I felt strong and healthy as I rolled Mason William Harkrader around Springfield in a wicker-backed wheelchair with a small wheel in back for balance. Many of the White citizens seemed wary, but most were polite.

"Why are you doing this?" he asked.

"It's a nice day. I thought you might be getting tired of looking at the same four walls."

"Taking me out every day won't change my mind," Harkrader said. "I still hate all you coloreds. You're the cause of the war. So many died. There was so much destruction."

"Should have stayed obedient little slaves, huh?" I asked.

"Exactly. You were taken care of."

I didn't say what I was thinking — that I had a plan to take care of him. Instead, I decided that I'd heard enough of young Harkrader's venom and sent him back to the fort in a wagon. I walked along the wooden sidewalks to clear my head. I would have to see his father soon. I might have to face him in a duel.

Someone grabbed me from behind, pinning my arms to my body in a bear hug. I leaned forward. I stomped my right foot down on his. He yelped. I slammed the back of my head into his face as hard as I could. My head ached, but I ignored it. His hug loosened enough for me to turn into him. I brought my knee up into his groin. He groaned and sagged, but he still held me. I backed up to a store wall behind me. My assailant grabbed my shirt with his left hand. He pulled back his right arm and swung a wild looping right fist at my head. I slapped his left hand off my shirt and slipped to the left just before his punch smacked into the front wall of the store.

My attacker crumpled to the sidewalk, writhing in pain. He extended his left hand, maybe trying to push himself up. When I brought my entire weight down on his hand, I heard a satisfying crack.

Breathing hard, I looked down at the fat, bloody-faced, bearded White man on the sidewalk. He wore a spotless Confederate uniform. A gray kepi cap rested on the sidewalk close to his head.

A tall, thin White man in a white apron stepped out of the store. He walked with a limp.

"I saw the whole thing," the storekeeper said. "He grabbed you without warning. I'll get the marshal."

I nodded. Buoyed by adrenalin and anger, I reached down, grabbed the waist of my attacker's trousers and the collar of his shirt, and lifted him over my head. I held him there for a moment before tossing him into the muddy street.

"Take your time," I said. "He's not going anywhere."

"Are you all right?" asked the storekeeper.

"I haven't felt this good in months."

"All the time I was in the war, I never saw me a fat Confederate," said the storekeeper. "Maybe there were some during the first weeks. I got drafted in after you Yanks killed off the hot heads eager to see the elephant. I never had enough money to avoid it like the big plantation owners who were slaveholders. The women wouldn't let me stay out of it. I never saw a uniform as clean as that neither. This parlor soldier might of been a home guard, but he did not ever cross a field while the bullets flew around him or watch a friend bleed to death."

"I'm sure you're right," I said. "I do wonder one thing about him."

"What's that?"

"I wonder if he has a good enough friend to wipe his ass for him."

The storekeeper tapped me on the shoulder and laughed.

. . .

Mica and Abraham Harkrader were waiting when we returned to the infirmary in the fort. Mica had the Whitworth with him.

"Mr. Harkrader, I promised to meet with you when my business was completed to see if you still want to duel. I hope you don't. Thank you for keeping your crew in check. More men would have died if you had not."

He gestured toward his son. "All my men stayed safe except for this bad apple. What do you plan to do with my son?"

"There will be a trial. He will be charged with attempted murder. If he shows up at the trial, I believe he will be found guilty and hung."

The elder Harkrader blinked. His lips trembled.

"I believe a murder trial would inflame divisions between Whites and Blacks regardless of the outcome. People are just starting to get to know one another. I'm thinking of sending him home to heal. But I don't want him to stick around very long."

"Why not?" demanded the younger Harkrader. "You're a woolly headed idiot. I don't think a jury of my neighbors would convict me. I am perfectly safe at home."

"'Less I skin you and nail your hide to the wall of the barn," said his father.

"You might be right about your neighbors, but I could hold your trial here. Besides," I told him, "you are in danger in Springfield."

"Why?" he sneered. "Do you think any pickaninny could kill me?"

"One almost did. But I am thinking about your Klan brothers. The Giant Monkey, or whatever you call your sergeant at arms and other high-ranking blowhards who were too cowardly to join in on the action— They've seen me push you around in the wheelchair. Like you, they don't think coloreds are smart enough to reckon their way out of an open door. I've heard rumors that they decided they were betrayed by one of their own. A White traitor. Only one of the attackers survived. How do you suppose those flea-bitten heroes figure that happened? And that he's the one gets pushed around in a wheelchair by me? Those geniuses have definitely sighted in on who the traitor was."

Mason William tried to lunge at me. He fell on the floor, groaning.

"Careful. You'll rip open your wounds," I said.

He sputtered, "You think you're so smart, don't you? I hear from my friends that a Klan sergeant-at-arms is in Springfield looking for you. They call him Bear 'cause he sneaks up from behind, grabs you in a hug, and pins your arms. Then he squeezes until your ribs break and stomps you to death. Maybe the marshal will get there in time so you'll end up still alive but stuck in a wheelchair like me."

"Maybe," I said. "Maybe not."

"I no longer wish to duel with you," said Harkrader. "I'll take this fool off your hands and send him away. You saved the lives of some of my men, including my son, worthless excuse for a man that he is. I am eternally in your debt. Can I see the rifle?"

Mica handed him the Whitworth. Harkrader examined it minutely and handed it back.

"Clean as a whistle, well cared for," he said. "I believe it is in good hands. Use it well."

. . .

I was getting to the tail end of my duties. Captain March was still missing, but the president had assigned other men to find him. He had not told me he was replacing me as the temporary commander. I guessed he would not bother.

I moved out of the hotel, which pleased Toby. I took over the commanding officer's office and replaced the shotgun that Wilber had taken and used, just in case. So far, looking through March's papers had yielded no clues to his whereabouts or any clear indication of his next steps.

The Ashmores started teaching inside the fort, which March had discouraged. Chaplain Wells, who was called Captain but paid as a lieutenant, worked with them. The soldiers were eager students. They were close at hand when Preacher Day from Springfield Presbyterian Church came calling. I invited them to join us. He knew the Ashmores. I introduced Chaplain Wells, not mentioning Wells' role in the army.

Day wore a facial expression that might have matched John the Baptist's when he ranted about sin.

"Who is in charge?" Day demanded.

"I am," I answered. "How may I be of service?"

"I have to chide you," he said.

"About what, sir?" I asked.

"You had the bodies of those you slew dumped on the grounds of my church."

"The bodies of the men who came in secret to kill the families who live here and burn their homes?" I asked. "The would-be murderers of women and children?"

"Those who died in iniquity, as the Bible described?" Chaplain Wells chimed in.

Day's gaze shifted to the chaplain.

"Um, yes," Day said.

"I gave the order for that," I said.

"That was ill done," said the preacher.

"Please tell me what would have been better," I said. "Some of those devils in human flesh were members of your church, I believe. Their families were able to hold funerals and claim whatever money or goods were on the bodies. Would it have been better for the families to wonder forever what happened to their menfolk? Or would it have been kinder to leave the bodies where they fell and force wives and children to search through a field of rotting corpses for their family members? Please advise me. What would you have done?"

Day opened his mouth and then closed it without saying anything. I let the silence stretch out.

"It was hard on the members of my church to have so many dead bodies around," said Day. "It was not fair for my congregation."

"Indeed, it was not," I said. "Just imagine what it was like for people here to see how many men tried to kill them. Not fair, not fair at all."

"My people were burdened with trying to console and comfort so many," the preacher persisted. "It's hard enough to care for our own. Do not put them under a strain like that again."

"I understand," said Wells. "You are telling us that your people are limited in the care and compassion they have for others. We are fortunate, indeed, that our Quaker brothers and sisters, although not members of any church, are able to open their hearts and minds to all in need."

"They are not baptized," snarled the preacher. "They do not take communion. They're going to hell."

"That may be," I said. "I claim no ability to decide in advance how God will act and no special knowledge about God's will. During the war someone asked the President if he thought God was on the side of the Union. He said, 'Sir, my concern is not if God is on our side. My greatest concern is to be on God's side, for God is always right."

"That man is an infidel," said Day.

"Sir, in the end, if I have a choice between your heaven and wherever Mr. Lincoln and these Quakers end up, I'll skip your heaven and go with them," I told him.

Day lowered his voice and growled, "Slaves, obey your masters."

Wells replied, "In Galatians we are told, 'There is neither Jew nor Greek, there is neither bond nor free, there is neither male nor female: for ye are all one in Christ Jesus.' And 'Stand fast therefore in the liberty wherewith Christ hath made us free, and be not entangled again with the yoke of bondage'."

"Even the devil can quote Scripture," said Day. "What gives you the right to interfere in the sacred bond between a man and his wife?"

"So, I guess now we have come to the real reason for your visit," I said. "Some women who are members of your congregation have come here on their own to escape from their abusive husbands. They came voluntarily. They are free to go at any time. I allow their husbands to come to visit them and try to persuade their wives to return home, but I will not continence anyone dragging off a woman against her will. As you no doubt know, law officers have talked with a number of the women and found nothing illegal in their staying here."

Day frowned.

"Your wife is not among the women. Not yet. My advice to you is — don't give her a reason to join the women here."

. . .

Early in the morning, Wilber and Hosea arrived, just before Toby and Bonnie. The Ashmores showed up too.

"Look at all the people I am indebted to," I said. "I guess I won't have to track down each one of you to express my gratitude. Thank you all. I imagine you have reasons to see me."

"Can I ask what thee plans to do once thy work is finished?" asked Jacob.

"I don't have any particular plans," I said. "In my experience, the future is always full of surprises. I imagine something will show up that requires my attention. It always has."

"Well, while you are still in charge, I'd like to see if we can reach some sort of agreement about my enterprises," said Wilber. "I know you don't work for me and what we decide may have a time limit on it, but I'd like to get some agreement that I can at least negotiate from in the future."

"There is no way that a white man can own property here," I said. "You built the buildings. You can keep any of them you can haul away on your back."

I was surprised that he smiled in response.

"That's what I thought. I have an idea. Facing losing all my businesses, I propose to sell the businesses, for a percentage of the on-going profits. The people who work there continue to work as employees. I'll get a smaller but ongoing and completely legal income."

"Interesting," I said. "I don't reject the idea out of hand, but I have many questions. First, who has enough money to buy your enterprises?"

"I'm not asking for money. I will give them away, knowing I cannot keep them. I will give them to the local government, with a force including veterans from the 54th Massachusetts Volunteer Infantry. The good people around nearby Fort Carney had a stable situation long enough that they had time to develop a government. They have a civilian mayor and city council and a court system based on the United States and state constitutions. They haven't figured out everything, but they have enough to start. Here Captain March was mayor, judge, and sheriff all rolled into one. What I'm proposing would change that."

I looked around. Nobody objected. "Go on," I said.

"It would be much easier to set up a government if there was money to pay a mayor, a law officer, and a judge. Fort Galloway will eventually be abandoned so there will be buildings and space but nothing more. I'm sure the people from Fort Carney will be willing to help, but an operating bank, hotel, and livery would be beneficial."

"Mr. and Mrs. Ashmore, thank you for being here," I said. "You have nothing to lose or gain from the proposal. Surprisingly, I find little on the negative side. Am I overlooking something?"

"We Friends favor our religious values over written laws and courts," said Jacob. "The war was hard for us because we are morally opposed to both violence and slavery, although some Friends did carry arms for the Union. I'll not say they were wrong. We do know some anti-slavery lawyers who would probably be happy to help thee set up thy system. I can't say I find the idea flawed, although as thee knows personally, the devil is in the details."

He smiled. His wife nodded.

"I favor the races working together, Mr. Wilber," I said, "but I would like it better if there was more than one White man involved."

"We thunk on that, too," said Hosea. "We know Whites what are int'rested in buyin' the rice, cotton, indigo an' sug'r bein' grown."

"That sounds too much like sharecropping," I said. "To get my support, at a minimum, they'll need to find partners among the settlers. And anyone who lives here is free to open their own business to compete."

"An' I know men that'd work 'longside fisherman, crabbers, and such. I know men'd work in da fields."

"That I like, Hosea," I said. "I brought four mules with me, knowing how much people need them. I'll let the government auction them off to add to their startup money. There are lot of details to be arranged, but for the short time I'm still here, I'll back your plan."

"That is another thing," said Bonnie. "We'd like you to stay on. We need a town marshal. People are grateful for all you've done."

I chuckled to myself as I thought about the concussion and that soft, comfortable bed in the hotel. "Maybe you could say I lit the fuse, but I missed the fighting. It was all of you who had to face the explosion. I have the feeling I'm nearly used up as a lawman. It's a wonder I'm still alive with all the mistakes I made. Maybe I should retire like President Lincoln."

"At least think about it," said Bonnie. "We need someone like you as mayor too. Don't turn us down until you sleep on it."

The group filed out. The Ashmores stayed behind. Jacob excused himself, and Raymond entered the room.

"I need to talk with thee," said Ruth. "I'm afraid I misled thee. When I told you about Lilly, I was too cynical. She is remarkable in many ways."

I nodded and said, "I agree. I admire her determination and intelligence. She has survived a terrible life. She did what she had to do. She has remade herself. And she is an amazing artist. I truly wish her well."

I looked at Raymond. He remained silent.

"She came to me," Ruth said. "She said thee are the first man ever who looked past her beauty. She would like to see thee and try to explain some things. She said she does not want anything more than a chance to talk. I think she is sincere. I believe I encouraged thee to view her harshly. I warned thee that she would immediately evaluate you in terms of how being with thee would help her rise in the world. And so she did at first. But after talking with her, I believe she sees thee as more than the next possible stepping stone on her path."

I looked at Raymond, who had stayed quiet.

"Raymond, I'm not comfortable with this talk in front of you. She's your wife. We've been talking about her as if you were not present. What do you think about this?"

"Ben, we ain't never jumped the broom. We ain't gonna be together much longer. True is I got wid her partly 'cause it makes other men think I'm somethin' special. I even grabbed dat dang shirt what got me in Dutch into town when she wasn't lookin,' meanin' to show off. You, Mica, and Click is the real special a man kin be. I dint fight in da war."

He shook his head. "I know I cain't talk wid her about stuff like what you and her talked 'bout. I'm tossing my cards in. I'm outta da game. I wish you and her well."

78

"Don't sell yourself short, Raymond. You stood up to the Dickensons."

"Friend Ben, thee once implied that thee valued my perceptions," said Ruth.

"Oh, I do indeed," I said.

"Please, as a personal favor to me, to untrouble my conscience, will thee be a true friend and go to her home to talk with her again? Thee are a good man. I can see the light of God in thee and in her too."

She had tears in her eyes. I sighed.

"I will. Today."

Since there was nothing that needed my immediate attention and I wanted to get the task over with, I headed to the livery. I spent a few minutes with each of the mules, thinking I would miss them as much as any person I met along the way.

I rented a horse, petted Darkee, and we set off toward the farm. People I passed waved and called out greetings, as if I had done anything more than my job. Darkee seemed happy for the chance to trot. I felt comfortable and close to what I had been physically before Hosea clobbered me. The weather was clear, and I enjoyed a rare sense of accomplishment.

I again noticed how the farm was built in a way that pleased the eye. I stood in the yard in front of the house and hollered, "Lilly, are you home?"

She came from the garden wearing an apron with dirt stains. Her face was smudged. Somehow the combination enhanced her appearance. Without trying, she was even more lovely than the last time I saw her.

"Ruth spoke with you and persuaded you to come?" she asked.

"Yes. I barely know the woman, but I feel like she's an old friend. I didn't want to disappoint her."

"Will you give me a moment and join me on the porch?"

"Of course."

I sat in a rocking chair and looked out over the farm. I didn't know how Lilly had laid out the plans for construction that resulted in such a sense of calm and peace. In a few minutes, Lilly appeared, having washed her face but still wearing the apron. She carried a tray with glasses on it.

"Would you care for some lemonade?" she asked.

"Thank you."

We sat in uncomfortable silence, not looking at each other. Several minutes passed, and then she sighed and spoke.

"Thank you for coming. This is difficult for me to say, but I failed to clarify certain things we spoke of before. I find that it matters to me that I allowed you to think about me as you seem to. I don't ask for anything except for your attention."

"I'm starting to believe that I was hasty in some matters concerning you," I said. "I fear that I unfairly judged you. I apologize for that."

"There is no doubt about my past. I have been used by many men to satisfy their lust."

She paused to look at me. I nodded.

"You don't despise me for that?" she asked.

"For being powerless? No. Why would I blame you for what was beyond your control?"

"A great many people do. Men especially. It made me hard and bitter. I admit I used some men to protect me from other men. I manipulated them heartlessly. I controlled men by using the accident of my beauty and light skin color."

"You cleverly used what God gave you," I said. "I have never been in a situation anything like that, but I have used misunderstandings and false implications to stay alive."

"When I go with a man, I always plan how to rid myself of him," said Lilly. "You were right to suspect that I made a shirt for Raymond that I knew would attract unwanted attention from jealous men. I knew Raymond was vain enough to ignore the danger and strut around like a tom turkey. He'd none nothing to harm me. In fact, he'd protected me from other men, yet I was ready to set him up, if the need came. I know all too well about jealous and prideful men."

"I was wrong to assume you had sent him to town to get killed," I said.

"Yes. He grabbed the shirt off the clothesline when I was not looking. I've lied many times but never to you. That's the truth. You were right to recognize that I had a plan to get him out of my life.

And it was a plan that could get him killed. I have no excuse. There is no justification for my past lies and wicked behavior."

"Honestly, that frightened me," I said. "You could do the same with me if I actually went with you."

Lilly's eyes widened.

"You thought about...us?"

I felt my face redden. "Don't, don't worry about it. Sort of a daydream. Impossible back then. I had to prevent a massacre. Anyway, Raymond did leave on his own. You didn't need to make him a shirt."

"That's true. Spending time with you and the soldiers gave him the chance to see what men worthy of respect are like. He was able to see that he never really liked me very much, but he did like the attention he got for being with me. Like men who get attention for owning the fastest horse in the territory. Attention gained not earned." She paused. "You really thought about being with me?"

"Imagination more than thought. Your persistence and how far you have advanced by force of will are incredible. No one looking at you would appreciate the grit you have. You could easily get by on your appearance alone, but instead you change yourself. You can see not just what is, but what could be. Like the setup of this farm. You have a remarkable sense of color." I had to look away. "But I had my duty. My purpose in life. It keeps me going and it is the only thing that makes sense about me being here and alive. How could I think about the future when might well die at any time? People kept trying to kill me. And you were involved with Captain March. What about that?"

A movement near the end of the porch caught my eye.

"Yes, do tell. What about that?"

A gaunt figure, dirty and dressed in rags, had sneaked up to the porch. I had been so engrossed in the conversation that I had not noticed. He held a Colt Army Model 1860 revolver, which was pointed at my heart.

"Why, Captain March, what a surprise," Lilly said sweetly.

"A surprise that I'm still alive? A surprise that I'm here as planned? I'm surprised to find you chatting like old friends with the man I hate worst in the whole world. I'm filthy, starving, nearly dying of thirst, but I'm here at last. Are you finally ready to come with me? No more last-minute excuses or delays?"

Lilly looked down and nodded her head.

He sneered at me.

"And you. No wonder they call you the devil. You're still alive even though I tried to kill you…how many times?"

My heart was pounding but I kept my voice steady. "I'd say four, but I'm not sure you should get credit for every attempt. You are not the only person who wanted to kill me. However, I am certain that things get worse for you every time you try. You really ought to give up trying. Disgraced, with men scouring the countryside for you. I'm not sure how much worse things can get."

March turned his head and spat.

"They haven't found me yet. My gold and silver are safe. My escape route is ready. The most beautiful woman in the world will come with me. I'd say, despite all the setbacks, I have done very well."

"Your plan was brilliant," I said. "I admit it. You certainly fooled me. Wilber and Hosea were clueless. You're very smart. I asked about you. The Union army wouldn't let you fight because you were the very best man available at logistics. You were tough enough to make it here without being detected. Bravo. But now you're on your own. You have to retrieve the money, get the transportation ready, and prepare yourself. You can't go looking like you do now."

He snorted and spat again. "For a colored man, you are quite clever. I regret that the Klan didn't get the chance to burn out the whole nest of parasites. Some of you are exceptional. Like Lilly. As you know, she gets in your blood and makes it hard to think about anything but her. And she isn't really a woman like you aren't really a man. You just have the outward shape. Maybe that's part of her enchantment or maybe she works voodoo. I don't know."

He shifted his gaze toward her. "Get the carriage. Is the money still in it?"

"Yes, sir," Lilly answered softly. She left the porch.

I kept looking at March. The rocking chair I sat in was not stable. Its arms made reaching my holsters awkward. He had not cocked the Colt. If I had been standing, I was pretty sure I could draw and kill him before I died. But there was no point in wasting time considering that.

"Are you quite certain Lilly is with you?" I asked.

"She bewitched you, like she has done with me and so many others," said March. "I have an advantage. I'm White. I know how to keep the Black race obedient. It's not pretty, but it works."

He stroked his chin. "I'm not sure what I should do about you," he said. "I could shoot you, but you're a tough son of a bitch. You might live long enough to pull a revolver and shoot me. I'm not going to get close enough for you to grab me."

"Killing me would upset my dog," I said. "Have you ever killed a man in cold blood? In battle it's hard enough. But if you haven't done it when your life is not at stake, you'd be surprised how hard it is for your mind to force your hand to shoot."

Lilly returned, leading a matched set of stately chestnut Morgan horses that were hitched to a well-appointed chaise carriage.

"Lilly, go unhitch his horse and send it off. It'll go back home on its own. Devil man, take one pistol out of its holster, open the cylinder, and drop it on the floor. Careful now."

His hand was shaking, but he was too close to miss. If he'd been determined to kill me, I would have been dead already. I did as he asked and heard the cylinder hit the porch.

"Good, now do the same with the other revolver."

I did as he directed me.

March smiled.

"I'm not going to kill you. Not at the moment. I don't care about you, but searchers take their work more seriously when looking for a killer. And that simpleton Grant is like a bulldog. He would never stop looking for me if I murdered one of his. For some reason he actually thinks coloreds are people. We'll be long gone by the time you walk back to town. We'll get a quick cleanup and a change of clothes. Nobody will stop a wealthy man and his mistress. Don't come after me or I will definitely kill you."

He got into the carriage and took up the reins. I heard them talking.

"Mistress? You said you'd marry me."

"Marry you? Eventually the madness in my blood will burn out.

I would never marry a former slave, let alone a whore. Maybe I'll keep you on after I escape your spell. It might be amusing to show you off to friends as a white-skinned former slave now condemned to be a scullery maid."

I heard a shot. March's body tumbled to the ground. A derringer landed on the ground beside him. Blood seeped from a wound in his temple.

"Did you hear that?" Lilly demanded. "The bastard would make me a scullery maid."

She jumped out of the carriage and stomped over toward me. Her eyes flashed. She whirled around, marched to the body and spat on the corpse.

"You wouldn't have gone with him, would you?" I asked.

"No, of course not. And I would have killed him if he made any attempt to kill you. He could never pass up the chance to show how smart he was. You kept him talking. He would never kill an appreciative audience."

"You were very convincing," I said.

"Men generally believe anything they want to. Now what? Will you arrest me and turn me in?"

She put her hands on her hips and glared at me. I carefully considered how to answer her question.

"Why in the world would I do that?" I asked. "I couldn't see anything from where I was and the voices were not entirely clear. I can only imagine how upsetting it must have been for you."

She frowned. "What?"

"Since I don't know what really happened in detail, and I'm an honest man, I can only use my imagination to assume you were shocked. March must have had a conscience when he explained that he could not live any longer with the evil he had committed before pulling out a derringer and shooting himself in the temple."

Lilly stared at me.

"You flew out of the carriage, highly upset. March's suicide must have been truly unnerving."

Lilly's shoulders shook. I didn't know if she was laughing, crying, or both.

"Truly, I've never seen anything like that before in my life," she said. "He died right in front of me. Terrible."

"I do have one request," I said. "If you ever want me to leave you, just tell me. I'll go. No need for a big fuss."

"What I want is for you to stay with me."

AUTHOR'S NOTE

I believe the history of the United States after the American Civil War would have been profoundly different if two events had not happened. First, the assassination of Abraham Lincoln deprived the nation of a masterful politician who spent the war being excoriated on one hand for moving too slowly toward emancipation, and on the other hand for moving too quickly toward ending slavery. He dragged his reluctant allies with him along the path he chose. He might have eased the reentry of former Confederates to the nation and protected Blacks as free people.

Andrew Johnson, who became president after Lincoln died, rescinded William T. Sherman's Special Field Order No. 15. Lincoln's Secretary of War Edwin M. Stanton and General Sherman met with twenty Black leaders, mostly Methodist and Baptist clergymen, to plan for emancipation. The ministers said they would like to have land that they could develop on their own that was set apart from Whites, who they thought would not leave them in peace if forced to live together.

As Reverend Garrison Frazier said, "The way we can best take care of ourselves is to have land and turn it and till it by our own labor...and we can soon maintain ourselves and have something to spare.... We want to be placed on land until we can buy it and make it our own. I would prefer to live by ourselves, for there is a prejudice against us in the South that will take years to get over. "

Four days later the field order was issued. A strip of coastline stretching from Charleston, South Carolina, to the St. John's River in Florida, including Georgia's Sea Islands and the mainland thirty miles in from the coast, was designated. Military protection was promised until residents could protect themselves. Roughly 400,000 acres of land was distributed to newly freed Black families in up to forty-acre segments. Within six months, 40,000 people who had been enslaved lived on 400,000 acres of coastal land. They used their skills and labor to make the land productive. They also set up their own civic and educational institutions. They established their own militia, planning eventually to be able protect themselves from the Klan.

Despite the objections of General Oliver O. Howard, the Freedmen's Bureau chief, President Andrew Johnson overturned Sherman's directive in the fall of 1865 after the war had ended, and returned most of the land along the South Carolina, Georgia, and Florida coasts to the planters who had originally owned it.

ABOUT THE AUTHOR

Warren Bull is an award-winning author with more than a hundred short stories in publication. He is the author of four novels: *Abraham Lincoln for the Defense, Abraham Lincoln in Court and Campaign, Heartland* and *Death Deferred*. His short story collections are *Murder Manhattan Style, Killer Eulogy and Other Stories,* and *No Happy Endings. Abraham Lincoln: Seldom Told Stories* is his nonfiction history collection. He is an active member of Mystery Writers of America and a lifetime member of Sisters in Crime with no hope of parole. He blogs on Fridays on the "Writers Who Kill" blog. His website is www.WarrenBull.com